ROBBIR

THE HARDY BREED

**Center Point
Large Print**

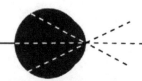

**This Large Print Book carries the
Seal of Approval of N.A.V.H.**

THE HARDY BREED

Giles A. Lutz

CENTER POINT LARGE PRINT
THORNDIKE, MAINE

This Center Point Large Print edition
is published in the year 2012 by arrangement with
Golden West Literary Agency.

Copyright © 1966 by Giles A. Lutz.
Copyright © 1973 by Giles A. Lutz
in the British Commonwealth.

First US edition: Doubleday and Company.
First UK edition: Collins.

The text of this Large Print edition is unabridged.
In other aspects, this book may vary
from the original edition.
Printed in the United States of America
on permanent paper.
Set in 16-point Times New Roman type.

ISBN: 978-1-61173-481-2

Library of Congress Cataloging-in-Publication Data

Lutz, Giles A.
The hardy breed / Giles A. Lutz.
pages ; cm.
ISBN 978-1-61173-481-2 (library binding : alk. paper)
1. Large type books. I. Title.
PS3562.U83H37 2012
813´.54—dc23

2012010425

CHAPTER ONE

This was old and bloody land. For almost two centuries five races had contested ownership of it: Americans, Frenchmen, Spaniards, Mexicans, and Indians. After all those years of contention it still belonged to no country, no race. Men tried to give it boundaries saying it was a strip one hundred miles wide running the length of the Sabine River. Other men denied promptly the legality of those boundaries. Consequently, it had no fixed law nor authority except that of the ruthlessly strong who made their own laws. The weak scampered through it like frightened rabbits—or perished.

It was called the Twilight Zone, and men crossed it in search of profits or in search of new homes. The lure of either had to be strong to make them venture into this wild country. It lay between Nacogdoches in the eastern part of the territory of Texas and Natchitoches on the Red River. A travesty of a road crossed the strip. Emigrants moving west toward the virgin lands of Texas ferried across the Mississippi at Natchez proved they had survived the bandits and footpads along the Natchez Trace. They skirted the bayou country, arrived at Natchitoches and took a deep breath before they ventured into the Twilight Zone. For the next hundred miles they would depend upon accurate weapons, vigilance, and prayers to see them safely through.

The western terminus of the road was at Nacogdoches, and Spanish merchants traveling the ancient road from Mexico City up through Saltillo and Monterrey then to Nacogdoches also took the same strained breaths and muttered the same prayers in another language. For they carried silver for purchase of merchandise in the United States. If they could get the merchandise back to Mexico the journey would show tremendous profits. If their gamble was bad they lost not only their silver but their lives.

The zone was peopled by the worst scum of several races. No country policed this land, and it was a robbers' haven drawing outlaws from Mexico, gamblers, murderers and thieves from New Orleans, pirates from the Gulf of Mexico, escaped slaves from the South, and criminals of all types from the United States. They lived in sod huts, log cabins, Indian tepees and lean-to's made of cane. They roved in bands forty to fifty strong and at times made deep forays into Louisiana stripping villages of everything they could carry away. But their easiest source of income was the travelers using the road between Natchitoches and Nacogdoches. Though the bands were loosely organized they were efficient. Informers worked for them from Natchez to San Antonio. Many a settler or merchant who had hired guards to see them safely across the zone would find they had hired the outlaws themselves. No man lived to speak of this, but the burned caravans and the bleaching bones were mute evidence.

The United States was too busy consolidating her purchase from France to be concerned about this narrow strip of land. For with the Louisiana Purchase in 1803 they had inherited a boundary dispute between Spain and France. The French once claimed land as far south and west as the Rio Grande. Spain claimed land as far east as the Mississippi River. France was embroiled with Great Britain, and Spain was having her troubles with the Mexicans' bid for independence. It was provident for each to back up in their claims leaving the Twilight Zone as a buffer between them. Now, neither country was concerned over the dispute. For Napoleon, needing money for his war against England, had sold the French claim to the United States, and the Mexicans had wrested their independence from the Spaniards. Someday either the United States or Mexico would have to police this strip, but now each was wary of stepping upon the other's toes.

The lone man sat hunched on the seat of the light wagon, his face turned from the driving rain. It had rained incessantly the last forty-eight hours, and the slicker was no longer protection against it. Moisture trickled in around the collar edges, and his body steaming under the almost airtight slicker sweated until he was as wet as though he rode with no protection. For two nights he had slept in damp blankets, and tonight would be no different. The team of horses slipped in the greasy footing, and the wagon lurched from side to side leaving twin snakelike tracks. Some of those ruts were six inches deep, and each time the horses seemed to struggle with greater effort the man tensed fearing the wagon would be stuck again. It had happened three times in the last twenty-four hours, and his shoulder was sore from lifting on the long pole he carried in the wagon to lift and pry an axle bogged deep in the mud.

Chichester Chaplin had cursed the weather until there were no more oaths left in him. He was a country man, patient with and used to the vicissitudes of the weather, but enough was enough.

He supposed he would have been wiser to have made camp before dark, but he had been impatient to reach Nacogdoches. He had hoped to make the town by tomorrow night, but with the road in this condition his hope was fading.

He resigned himself to the thought that another day would make no real difference. Haden Edwards might grumble at the delay, but then Edwards was always in a hurry in whatever he did. Edwards couldn't be blamed for his impatience this time, however. The light wagon

8

was loaded with gunpowder and lead, and the little colony in East Texas needed them.

"He ought to be glad that I get there at all," Chaplin grumbled aloud. He grinned as he heard his voice. Long hours of solitude did that to a man. It built a hunger in him for the sound of any voice, even his own.

The horses were moving at a dragging walk. The wise thing was to rest them, get what sleep he could then push on to an early start in the morning. His belly rumbled telling him that it had been many hours since he had eaten. The team must be weakening too for lack of food. He thought with a bleak assay at humor, the horses didn't lack for water.

He would be relieved when the journey was behind him. He had been warned how foolhardy it was for a lone man to attempt the crossing of the Twilight Zone. His ears had been filled with gruesome tales of ambush, torture, and murder. Not that he doubted the stories for he had seen the evidence of their truth with his own eyes. But Edwards couldn't spare enough men or wagons to make up a train to Natchitoches, and, at Natchitoches, Chaplin found that no train would leave for Nacogdoches for two or three months. Perhaps Edwards' fretting for the needed supplies had influenced Chaplin to volunteer, or perhaps he still felt it necessary to impress his father-in-law. He felt quite sure Edwards had never fully forgiven him for marrying Talitha. He had argued against Talitha's fear of his going, that a lone, light wagon could travel faster and be less conspicuous. He doubted he had convinced her for he hadn't fully convinced himself. But most of the trip was behind him, and he was safe enough.

He wasn't scoffing at the dangers. They were very real. Only this morning he had passed the ashes of a burned-out train. The rain left him no way of knowing how long ago it had happened for the ashes were sodden. But the state of the fourteen bodies told him it couldn't have been more than a few days ago. He had stared grimly at the stripped, mutilated bodies. Not all of the mutilation had been done by wild animals. And if any women had been traveling with the small train they had been carried away. Mexicans or Spaniards, he decided, looking at the faces. He could do nothing of real value for them. He had a shovel, but digging fourteen graves was a monstrous task for a lone man. Besides nothing could hurt them any more. He had shrugged and put his team into motion again.

The horses slogged through the heavy, holding mud, their heads drooping lower with each step.

Chaplin said, "Ho, Bess. Ann. Not much longer now."

The animals needed rest, and he wanted a fire and warm food. He had venison in his wagon from the deer he had killed this morning, but raw venison was singularly unattractive. But even if he could get a fire started in this rain it would be foolhardy. A fire could be seen for miles across this flat land, and it would be a beacon demanding investigation. The horses sloshed through a small creek, and a thought occurred to him. If he could find the spot he wanted he might have his fire and safety too.

He turned the team and followed the course of the creek, driving a thousand yards or better before he stopped. The bend just ahead of him looked as though it might be the spot he wanted, and he checked it out on foot. He grunted with the effort of the first few steps, for hours of riding a hard seat didn't make for pliant muscles. His weight came down heavily on his heels, and his buttocks were sore. It took a dozen steps to return any semblance of fluidity to his muscles.

Even with the rain the creek was carrying no great volume of water, but in some past time the width of its bed showed that it had. It was much wider here at the bend, and a great force of water had cut at the near bank and undermined it before the water straightened again. It left a thick overhang of earth over the six-foot indentation, and a man of Chaplin's height could stand erect in the shallow cave. The past high water had deposited a small amount of driftwood, and the overhang kept most of the rain from the wood.

He said, "Ah," as he felt the wood. It was damp,

but by gathering the small tufts of dried grass lodged in the twigs and branches he might be able to get a fire started and nurse it into larger life.

He returned to the wagon and led the team into a copse of small trees. He stripped the harness from them, and as he worked water from the limp, sodden leaves dripped down his neck. He picketed the horses and gave them a feed of grain. He heard their soft, nickering sigh as he fastened on the feed bags. The grass was lush in this country, and even in the timber he could feel its lengthy wetness wrap around his ankles. After the horses finished the grain he would remove the feed bags, and they could graze their fill. They would get all the moisture they needed from the wet grass.

He took coffee, a pot and cup and a haunch of venison from the wagon. He slung a blanket roll over his shoulder, debated upon taking the rifle and decided to leave it in the wagon. He had a pistol in the waistband of his trousers, and in the seclusion of the cave it should be more than enough. He picked up the gold-headed walking stick from the seat of the wagon. It was like an extension of his right arm, and he was rarely without it.

He moved back to the cave, gathered a tiny pile of the dried grass and lit it. He fed in additional wisps carefully to strengthen the flame, then added small twigs. He was a man of infinite patience when it need be, and he watched the growing fire with absorbed attention. He nodded in pleased satisfaction at the growth of his fire.

He straightened and stepped back. He slipped out of the slicker, careful that no flying moisture from it touched his fire. He was an incongruous figure in this wilderness. His painful thinness made him look taller than he was. The face was young, and a casual observer might think it on the weak side. A keen observer would notice that the gray eyes were set deep and had a bright alertness, almost a wary animal's alertness. He was in his twenties though the flickering firelight made him look older. He wore tight, doeskin trousers, a sharply cut blue coat, and a flowing silk cravat. A pearl-gray topper sat jauntily on his head. One might expect to see someone dressed like this walking down Canal or Bourbon streets in New Orleans or stepping into Connelly's Tavern on Gilreath's Hill in Natchez—but not here.

He looked at his coat and uttered a soft oath. It was limp from the moisture, and mud crusted its cuffs. He picked at the mud, and it wasn't set enough to come away cleanly.

He hunkered down beside his fire again. His expression wasn't as much hostile as it was withdrawn. Long ago he had learned not to trust too many people. From boyhood his name and appearance had been against him, bringing out the jeering cruelty in others.

He had been named after the town of Chichester

in England, and a thousand times as he was growing up he wished his parents had picked a less complex name. Now, it didn't matter to him at all. He could have changed that first name, and he kept it out of a perverse stubbornness. He had learned early that he accepted taunts, or he fought. And the better he fought the less bruises he received, and the quicker he shut up the taunters. Talitha accused him of liking to fight, and he had protested he had never looked for trouble. He didn't have to. It seemed to come looking for him, and he had never learned to sidestep it. A few people could put a warmth into those gray eyes, and when the warmth kindled a smile his face came alive and vibrant. He had a big mouth with strong, white teeth. By convention's standards he supposed he was a rebel, but a man had to follow his own dictates.

He fed heavier branches into the fire. The warmth grew and penetrated his wet clothing, and the little cavity was filled with the disagreeable smell of sodden material drying. He didn't have enough driftwood to keep a fire going too long, but he should be fairly dry by the time he curled up to sleep.

He dipped water from the creek and set the coffeepot on the edge of the coals. He cut strips from the venison haunch and impaled them upon the end of a sharpened stick. He held them over the fire, and his belly rumbled as the meat juices dropped and spluttered in the flames. He watched in complete absorption as the meat browned. He had the trait of a steady man, the faculty of shutting out everything but the task in which he was occupied.

He poured the coffee, tasted it, and made a wry face. It wasn't hot, and it was strong enough to carry the pot back to the wagon. He used his knife point to carry the strips of meat to his mouth. The meat would taste better with salt, but he decided against making a trip to the wagon for it.

The haunch had been whittled almost to the bone by the time he finished his meal. He poured tobacco from a small pouch into the battered bowl of a pipe, picked a burning stick out of the fire and lit the pipe. He belched comfortably as he leaned back against the earthen wall. He grinned as he thought of some of the meals he had eaten in fine homes. Such behavior as a belch would have shocked the guests at those dinners. That was one of the restrictions of being raised a gentleman. A man could rarely follow his natural impulses.

A branch burned through and broke, scattering the bed of coals. He poked the fire back together with the tip of his walking stick and squirmed his shoulders and hips into a more comfortable position on the gravelly soil. It was odd how little a man really needed for creature comforts, yet he demanded so much. Location had something to do with it, he thought soberly. Here in this untamed

15

land what he had tonight was riches. In Natchez it would be nothing.

He fed another branch into the fire. His supply of dry wood wouldn't last much longer. It didn't matter. He was almost dry. He would sleep comfortably tonight. He listened and thought the rain was lessening.

His eyes were closing in drowsy contentment when a voice came from out of the rainy darkness.

"Hold it real easy, mister. Or you're a dead man."

CHAPTER TWO

The voice came from the opposite bank of the creek, and it was as stunning as the impact of a club. For a moment Chaplin was certain he was having a bad dream. He jerked to a sitting position and waited for the bad moment to pass.

"That's smart," the voice said.

A bullet *thwocked* into the earth beside him, and he felt the stinging dirt through the material of his coat.

"That's to show you we aren't fooling. The next one will open up your head."

Chaplin remained motionless, but he was quivering inwardly with rage and helplessness. He cursed his stupidity in building a fire, he cursed his lapse into negligence. He had no illusions as to what could happen to him. He was in the Twilight Zone.

"That's behaving real nice," the voice said.

A second voice said eagerly, "Didn't I tell you, Rezin? Didn't I tell you I saw a fire as I passed by here?"

Rezin said dryly, "I'll praise you after I see what he's got. I'm coming across, mister. Haze will cover me. He shoots bettern I do."

Chaplin remained motionless as he heard the sounds of a descent down the opposite bank. He could do nothing else.

He heard the splashing of water as Rezin crossed the creek. The man stepped into the reach of the firelight, and he was unbelievably dirty. Chaplin was dirty but not like this. His was the honest dirt of travel without adequate facilities to remove it. Rezin's was the dirt of indifference, and the accumulation looked to be weeks old. He was a big man, and most of his face was covered with a thick, unkempt growth. His eyes glowed red in the firelight looking like the wild eyes of an animal peering out of deep brush.

"Come on across, Haze," he called. His eyes inventoried Chaplin's possessions. He said, "You won't believe what we've got. We've got a damned dude." He didn't know what they could do with the clothes, but there was a team and wagon in the woods. It wouldn't be a bad fifteen minutes' work at all.

Haze crossed the creek, and he was as dirty as Rezin. His ragged clothing was soaked, and he said in complaint, "I was wet enough without that wading."

He stared at Chaplin, and his jaw sagged. "What is it, Rezin?"

Rezin grinned. "It's plain to see you never saw a gentleman before. This came straight out of New Orleans."

"They wear clothes like that?"

Rezin nodded solemnly, but his eyes were filled with wicked amusement. "He's pretty near your size, Haze. You'd cut quite a figure in them clothes in Nacogdoches."

"Hell, they'd run me out of town," Haze protested. But he was intrigued with the idea. His eyes were fascinated with the topper and remained fixed on it.

"I'll take the slicker. I been needing one for a long time."

Rezin shook his head. "I already got my name on it."

"Goddam it, I got a choice," Haze said shrilly. "I found him first. You'd bust the shoulder seams."

Rage was blinding Chaplin. They were cutting him up before he was even dead. He sat quietly, his burning eyes watching their every move. He could do nothing else—not with two rifles covering him.

"Stand up and step out here," Rezin ordered. "And be damned careful." He knew his way around in a matter like this. He had no intention of entering the cramped enclosure while the dude was in it.

Chaplin's grip tightened on the tip end of his walking stick. He stood and moved out of the cave, his hands held over his head.

Rezin stepped back a pace. It was going to be difficult to catch him in a mistake.

"You're wasting your time," Chaplin said. His voice had a tendency to break, and the stick in his hand shook like a slender branch in a high wind.

Rezin's eyes danced with malicious delight. "I believe we got a scared pilgrim on our hands, Haze. Take that gun out of his pants."

Haze shifted his rifle to his left hand. He took two confident steps. He had nothing to fear from this frightened man. He reached for the pistol in Chaplin's waistband, and the stick held aloft came alive. It descended in a slashing arc catching Haze across the wrist.

Haze screamed in sudden pain and shock. He dropped the rifle, and caught his injured wrist in his hand. He staggered back a step, and Chaplin's shoulder dipped and hit him in the chest propelling him into Rezin. The unexpectedness of it momentarily froze Rezin. By the time he forced his tardy senses into alertness Haze was into him hampering the swing of his rifle.

Rezin swore and tried to throw Haze from him. The rage-contorted face springing at him froze his veins. The stick made its lethal slash again, and Rezin tried to duck it. He was too slow for even that.

The stick made a monstrous sound against his head. It sounded like an overripe melon being suddenly split. There wasn't even time for Rezin's opened mouth to squall its terror. His leg bones melted, and he dropped. He looked limp and broken and as he hit the ground blood was spurting across his forehead.

Chaplin didn't waste a second glance on him. He knew the deadly weight of that stick. He swung around, and Haze backed before him still holding his wrist.

"Don't," he begged. "We wasn't really going to do you any harm. You already broke my wrist. Isn't that enough?"

In proof he let go of the wrist, and it dangled grotesquely. His lips went white with the pain, and he seized it again in support of it.

"My God, mister," he whimpered. "You wouldn't hurt a wounded man." He backed with each word until the creek bank stopped him. His face was sick with fear, and the fear said he thought this man would hurt a wounded man.

His words broke off into a shrill, rising scream, and he turned and tried to run.

Chaplin took a long bound after him, and the stick struck again. The heavy knob caught Haze across the back of the neck, and his head seemed to have no connection with his body as he plunged forward on his face.

He flopped about as he fell into the creek, but there was no coordinated movement in him, only the reflex action of life draining away. He made one final heave, raising his body almost to his knees, then was still.

Chaplin leaned against the bank and panted heavily. Even after the panting subsided the killing fury remained in his face. He looked at the bodies, and there was no remorse in his eyes. Those two would never stop and murder another traveler.

He searched them and removed pistols from their holsters and knives from their boot tops. He added the rifles to the little pile. The knives had good edges, but the pistols and rifles were antiquated, but they were still weapons and so valuable.

He put on his slicker and gathered up his belongings. He would have to make a second trip for the guns and knives. He rehitched his team and at their protesting snorts said, "I'm sorry. But there might be more of them around." He had made one mistake, and it had almost cost him his life.

He started to climb into the wagon when he thought, they probably had horses. He hated to stumble about in the darkness looking for them, but horses were more valuable than weapons. And

21

if Haze and Rezin had tethered them the animals would stand out here and die of hunger and thirst.

It took him fifteen minutes to find the animals, then only the sound of an impatient hoof stomping the ground located them for him. He untied the reins from the small trees and led the animals toward his wagon. As he passed the little depression in the opposite bank he could see the wink of the fading fire. Haze and Rezin's obituary wouldn't last much longer.

Chaplin thought soberly it was odd how chance changed men's lives. By chance Haze had been at the right angle to spot the fire. Chaplin amended the original thought. Chance didn't really change those two's lives. It ended them.

CHAPTER THREE

In 1825, Nacogdoches was a hundred and eight years old, and it looked every minute of its age. Its one street was a muddy morass with water standing fetlock-deep in the ruts. Its log cabins were crumbling, its sod huts washed out, its few stone structures roofless. It looked like a tired, old woman with the seamy lines of experience cut deeply into her face, a woman who had seen the worst and expected no improvement. It had been kicked around, torn apart, and scattered. A less tough town would have perished years ago. But Nacogdoches had one advantage that marauding outlaws, Indians, and armies could not erase. It was the natural port of entry on the overland trail into Mexico. And over that trail poured the trade of two countries.

Trade was a weed that had stubborn roots. It could be chopped out, hacked down, or trampled, but let it be watered by the faintest hope of profits, and it flourished again. The original town was founded by Spanish missionaries, and Indians wiped it out. The Americans, needing only the slightest excuse for waging a virtuous war, had decimated the Indians. The Spaniards, considering it still their town, had returned and ran the Americans out. The town was built on violent land, and the blood of four races fed the rebellion seething in its soil.

Rebellion bred rebellion until Nacogdoches had known far more bloody years than peaceful ones. The last invasion was three years ago when the Spanish Loyalists, hating the sound of the word revolutionist, had swept the town clear of Mexicans, Americans, and Indians. They reasoned that with the town lying so close to the United States border anyone living here was infested with ideas of freedom. They left Nacogdoches in its present state, beaten and battered with sullenness replacing the spirit of hope. Few respectable citizens lived here or near it. Only the freebooters dared to take up residence in it for by the very nature of their trade they were transient men, and moving was no appalling thought to them. Being transient, the improvement of a town's appearance was the last thought to enter their minds.

Haden Edwards finished his inspection of the wagon camp at the east side of town. It was clean and orderly in marked contrast to the town though the sanitation facilities were becoming strained. He sniffed the slight stink in the air. He was going to have to do something about that. It was no small problem, the guarding of life and health of fifty-odd families. And the problem would grow. For more families were coming. Soon they would stretch from Nacogdoches to Natchitoches, a long, solid rope of them snaking across the empty prairies.

He walked with a heavy step, and his shoulders drooped. His belt struggled to confine his paunch. He was at the age when most men were thinking of retirement, and here he had taken on this vast project. When weariness' burden became over-powering he was quite certain he must be crazy. His wife told him so often enough. He couldn't blame her, he thought wryly. He had yanked her from the serene, well-ordered plantation life of Louisiana to this.

His body may have looked old and defeated, but the spirit that shone through his eyes never knew those weakening things. It stayed young and bright under the belaboring of every misadventure. The good Lord knew he had had enough of that in the past three years. But the dream was beginning to take solid form. Just these families being here was proof of that.

The wagons made a solid bulwark around the camp, and armed men patrolled that ring. They complained about the monotonous chore of it, but Edwards never eased on the order.

His eyes darkened as he saw the rifle leaning against the tail gate of a wagon. Its owner wasn't in sight, and Edwards filled his lungs.

"Stevens," he bellowed. "Jed Stevens."

He swung an angry face toward the man emerging from a tent. He strode toward him and demanded, "Where in the hell have you been?"

Stevens was a lank man with an overprominent nose and vague eyes. He kept shaking a lock of hair from his eyes. It never occurred to him to resent Edwards' rough tone. "I just stepped out of the sun for a minute, Mr. Edwards. It gets damned hot and tiresome just walking around doing nothing."

Edwards seized his arm and pulled him toward the spot he had vacated. "And left your rifle behind you," he growled.

"I didn't see no sense wagging it clear over to my tent and back," Stevens protested.

Edwards made a noble effort and contained his wrath. "Jed, it's important we guard this camp every minute." He pointed to a dozen men not fifty feet from the outside of the wagon ring. They stood there talking and spitting tobacco juice, and the ground at their feet was becoming sodden with it. A couple of them were in fringed buckskin, the leather stiff and black with grease and sweat. Several wore homemade jeans of brown Holland cloth, the material tougher than canvas and just about as stiff and awkward. A pair of doeskin pants and a yellowed linen shirt were in the group, stolen from some gentleman. Hats ranged from broad-brimmed felts to coonskin caps to a simple bandanna handkerchief knotted at each of its corners. All of them were bearded, and if one was near enough he would see the scale and pimples dotting their faces. Washing was a troublesome chore and to be avoided as much as possible. They chewed tobacco because matches were a luxury. Smoking was reserved for evenings and mornings when the coals of an open fire were available.

Stevens had no interest in the group. "They're there every day."

Edwards' temper bubbled and simmered and pushed hard at the lid he imposed on it. "Do you know why they're there? To see if there's something they can steal. Why one of them didn't slip in here and grab your rifle and run—" He shook his head. "They'd give a lot to replace their old flintlocks with one of our new cap and ball rifles."

Stevens looked properly impressed. "Shucks, Mr. Edwards, I didn't think about that."

"Never get careless about them, Jed," Edwards

26

said. "Any one of them would slit your throat for the boots you're wearing. One little slip on your part, and somebody in the camp could lose his life."

Stevens shifted nervously. The responsibility was enormous. "I won't forget," he promised.

Edwards sighed inwardly. Stevens wouldn't until the ennui of monotonous hours dulled him again. There was nothing to be gained by raising too much hell with him. Stevens was a simple, honest man doing the best he could with his capabilities.

Edwards slapped him on the shoulder and said, "I know you won't, Jed."

He started to move on around the ring, and Judge Williams called to him from across the enclosure. "You need a bracer, Haden."

Edwards crossed to him and stopped before the tent. "I need something," he said heavily. "Some-times I wish—" He let a sigh finish for him.

"That you'd never left Louisiana." Williams gave him a sympathetic smile. "You're carrying a heavy load for one man. I just opened a bottle of El Paso brandy. It'll lift your spirits."

Edwards sat down and gratefully accepted the tin cup. He said, "Whoa," as Williams splashed it half full. He sipped at it and said a pleasured, "Ah."

"What was that all about over there?" Williams asked curiously.

"Jed feels he can leave his post when he gets tired of it. Nothing *has* happened, and to him that means nothing *will* happen." Edwards frowned. "That attitude is going to get some of these people killed." He shook his head, and there was a defeated quality to the gesture. "I tried to weed out the incompetents, Judge, before I signed them up. But the plain truth is that if a man is doing well in the States he's not going to pull up his roots and come here. I've got some shiftless and irresponsible ones. They believe they can come out here and sit, and it'll make them rich where it didn't in the States."

A faint smile moved Williams' lips. He was a frail, bent-shouldered man with thinning, white hair. His face was a curious mixture of sympathetic planes and tough angles. "I signed up with you."

Edwards grinned wryly. "You know what I'm talking about." He could talk to Williams. They were of an age, and their minds met. "After all those years on the bench you earned your chance to get away from New Orleans' cold, damp winters."

"Didn't you earn your retirement, Haden?"

"Three years ago I thought I had." His eyes were beginning to fire. They always did when he spoke of his dream. "Then I heard of land at practically no cost. Millions of acres of virgin land, Judge. Unless you've crumbled land in your hands, unless you've planted seeds in it you don't know what news like that can do to a man."

"I guess I don't," Williams murmured. He had come here because of his health, but all these other people were here because of that invisible pull Edwards was speaking of.

"The Mexican government had all these empty acres," Edwards continued. "They wanted to fill them with energetic Americans, they wanted the tax money those Americans would make them."

Edwards was in a talkative mood, and Williams let him go on though he had heard something of this before. He knew Edwards was an *èmpresario*, a land contractor empowered by the Mexican government to bring in families and sell in turn land given him by the Mexicans.

"Judge, do you know what I see when I look out over this land?" Edwards said. "I don't see a decayed town filled with rotten scum. I see a clean, well-ordered city with neat homes and prosperous stores. I see great fields of cotton and pastures dotted with grazing cattle. I see prosperity for everyone and a better type of civilization than what we left behind." His breathing was a little heavier, and his face was flushed. "And I'll make it all come true."

Williams looked at him with faintly troubled eyes. He knew human nature. He should have after all those years on the bench observing every rough facet of it. Haden Edwards was a dreamer, a visionary of the most extraordinary nature. Did he have enough practicality, enough patience to make his vision come true? So far he had accomplished a great deal, but only the surface had been scratched. A million little things would continue to arise just like that irritating incident with Stevens. Would Edwards' explosive nature continue to take them in stride, or would the combined weight of them break him? It was going to be interesting watching the unfolding of the answer.

"Will the two cultures blend, Haden?" he murmured.

"The Mexicans are a shiftless lot," Edwards said contemptuously. "They'll blend with our ways, or they'll get out. I'll have to change a great many things. It took me three years to get my contract, and I had to accept some things I didn't like."

He was silent a moment thinking of those three years. He had suffered three years away from his family living in a strange country, and his resolution had never weakened. He had watched several revolutions in Mexico sweep away his negotiations with the incumbent government, and he had patiently started again. But he had come away with his grant. The land terms were so generous that the imagination could scarcely encompass them. For each one hundred families brought in, Mexico would give an *èmpresario* nearly five hundred thousand acres. A family that

30

wanted to ranch would get a *sitio*, and a *sitio* was over forty-four hundred acres. A family that wanted to farm would get a *labor* or a hundred and seventy-seven acres. The land would be given to the family free except for twelve cents an acre that the *èmpresario* could charge for his administrative costs. For those hundred families brought in, Mexico would give the *èmpresario* a grant of twenty-three thousand and forty acres. All land was to be tax free for ten years.

Edwards shook his head, and the memory of the three years faded. "I had to accept some things in my contract I don't like. I don't like the clause that all settlers become Catholic and learn the Spanish language. I don't like accepting their form of government for our cities. But I can raise my own army for defense. And I have full authority over the land within my grant."

It was a staggering amount of responsibility and power to be given one man—and to be given by a foreign government. Williams wondered if the Mexican government knew they could be opening a Pandora's box.

"Won't there be legal titles already issued within your grant?" Williams asked.

Edwards frowned. Evidently, it was a sore point with him. "Maybe a few," he admitted. "I'll have to honor any titles given either by the old Spanish government or the new Mexican Republic."

The sweep of his hand wiped out the town of

Nacogdoches. "Can you imagine any of those wretches out there owning title to anything?"

"But you'll check them out?" Williams insisted.

"You bet I'll check them out," Edwards said grimly. "And if they produce a title out they go."

Williams foresaw much trouble ahead. Squatters who had lived on their land for many years grew to think of that land as their own. They would resist expulsion. He was quite certain that Edwards would meet that resistance with violence.

"Did the Mexican government give other contracts?" he asked.

"Stephen Austin got a claim for five hundred families," Edwards said indifferently. "Green De Witt received one for three hundred families."

His indifference whetted Williams' curiosity. He had never heard just how much land Edwards had received. "And yours?" he asked softly.

Pride was in Edwards' grin. "Eight hundred families. And when I have them all here I'll go and ask for more land."

Williams could say one thing for Edwards. The man dreamed big. And he just might have enough drive and determination to pull it off.

"Could you have had your choice of land other than this?" he asked.

Edwards laughed. "I could. I know what you're thinking. You're wondering why I picked land already infested with scum. Because it's closest to the States. Because new arrivals will see a prospering colony here and have no desire to go on to De Witt or Austin."

Williams nodded in admiration. If Edwards' colony succeeded he would probably pick off a lot of De Witt's and Austin's families. But Austin and De Witt had one big advantage. They didn't have the squatter problem Edwards had asked for.

"Will there be other *empresarios*?"

Edwards' teeth flashed. "They'll flood in here after we make a go of it and show them the way. But one was turned down while I was in Mexico City. A Dr. Hunter. I don't know where he got the title. He's part Cherokee, and he wanted no land for himself. He wanted it for his people, the Indians. He asked for the northern half of Texas saying his families were already there. He got nothing."

"I know one thing," Williams said slowly. "You're going to need all the help you can get."

"I've got the best in the world," Edwards replied, and his grin broadened. "I've got Chichester.

"You don't think so?" He challenged the doubt in Williams' eyes. "I didn't think so either when I first saw him. Talitha married him while I was in Mexico City. When I got back and saw him I wanted to pitch the damned fortune hunter out on his tail. I did just like you're doing. I judged him on his appearance." His voice was musing.

"There's something special in that boy. Hardy, I guess you'd call it. Yessir, he belongs to a special breed of man."

Williams' eyes were bright with interest. "What changed your mind about him?"

"We were held up on the Natchez Trace by a couple of footpads. Chichester looked like he was going to shake to pieces at the sight of those pistols. I was so ashamed of him that I could feel its sourness coming up in my throat. You know that stick he always carries? He used it. He split a head and broke an arm. One footpad was dead, and the other ran howling up the Trace."

"It's hard to believe," Williams murmured.

"He'll fool most people. But Talitha saw something in him. He didn't fool her."

Williams said, "I haven't seen him for several days. Where is he?"

"He went back to Natchitoches for a new supply of powder. When Ames overturned his wagon in that creek he ruined most of what we had."

"He didn't go alone?" Williams said in disbelief.

"He insisted. I traveled alone to Mexico City and back. He said he could make it alone to Natchitoches and back." Edwards chuckled. "I think he's still trying to impress me."

"My God, man," Williams said. "You don't seem worried."

"I'm not. He got in a couple of hours ago. He's with Talitha."

"He didn't have any trouble?" Williams asked.

"He says he didn't. But he brought back a couple of extra horses and a brace each of rifles, pistols, and knives. He ran into trouble someplace. But you can't get much out of Chichester unless he wants to talk." He stood and stretched. "Two hours is long enough for any man. I've got to put him to work. By the way, he's an excellent surveyor."

Williams laughed. "It sounds as though you couldn't have done better if you had hand picked him."

"I couldn't," Edwards answered. "He's quite a—" He never finished. His frowning attention was on the man hurrying toward them. The man's haste said emergency.

The man stopped and said breathlessly, "Mr. Edwards, we may have trouble. A couple of those toughs are at the picket line claiming that two of those horses Mr. Chaplin brought in are stolen."

"He's with his wife. Go get him," Edwards ordered.

"Somebody must have told him. He's already there."

Williams noticed how bright Edwards' eyes had grown. The prospects of trouble was a tonic to some men.

"Come along, Judge," Edwards said. "This might be interesting."

Williams stood. "I wouldn't miss it for the world," he said.

CHAPTER FOUR

The room was filled with people, yet Captain Jim Gaines looked as though he was alone. He had the faculty of withdrawing from people, of erecting an invisible wall that none of them dared attempt to breach. He was a big man in size, but he was big in his ability to hold dominion over other men. That coupled with a complete ruthlessness gave him sway over the Twilight Zoners. At times even his stomach turned at the men he must work with, but he never let the weakness dilute practicality. He was a wealthy and respected man. He wasn't sure how much land he owned, but it stretched far beyond the eye's reach in every direction from Nacogdoches. Now, Haden Edwards was a threat to that land and to Gaines' standing, yet it caused him no real concern. He had run out tougher men than Edwards had ever thought of being—run them out or shot them down. Edwards could take his choice.

He had earned his land, and nobody was going to take it away from him. He had ridden into East Texas in 1812 under the West Pointer Augustus Magee. He jeered at the memory of Magee. Now there was a man of principle—and where was he today? Gaines neither knew nor cared. He could be certain of one thing. Magee hadn't grown wealthy on his Army pay. Magee came to protect

Americans living in Nacogdoches and stayed to help the Mexican revolutionists sweep the Spanish planters out of the country. That had been a gay, reckless time with no real danger. For few of the Spaniards offered any real resistance. They had ridden up to hacienda after hacienda finding them deserted. Gaines remembered the looting of them, the wanton destruction of everything that couldn't be carried away.

All those empty haciendas had given him an idea. They were there simply for the claiming. And he had claimed until the thought of more land had no appeal. After the revolution a few of the planters dared to return. They found Gaines in possession of land and hacienda. He had simply killed the unreasonable ones, the men who had insisted that the land still belonged to them. Now, Haden Edwards was saying that everyone must have a legal title to his land. Jim Gaines had his title all right—his determination to hold his land backed by the guns of the Twilight Zoners.

A burst of laughter broke into his thoughts. He swung around from the window and swept the faces of the half-dozen men in the room. He knew the laughter wasn't at him. Not a man here was that daring.

"What's funny?" he demanded.

"Fanstow says he knows where he can get him a clean, linen shirt," Sugg drawled.

Big Sugg was a mulatto, and his dark ancestors showed in his thick features. His voice was soft and slurred. He looked completely harmless, but those wild eyes gave him away. Gaines had seen him squeeze the life and breath out of three men. He was wanted back in the States, for what crime Gaines didn't know. He suspected a man could name any one of a dozen, and it would fit Sugg.

Gaines glanced at Fanstow. The linen shirt he wore was a dirty gray. It should be after the months of steady wearing. Fanstow never thought of having it washed. The shirt would probably dirt rot and drop off his back.

"I sure do," Fanstow said. He was a little man with the bright, beady eyes that went with a weasel face. He picked at a flake of scale on his chin with a thumbnail. He had a deep aversion to water, and the smell of him made that aversion known.

Gaines remembered when Fanstow had stripped that shirt off a body. The man liked the feel of the material against his skin. It might be the only one of its kind he would ever own for very few men wearing linen shirts rode into the Twilight Zone.

"Where?" Gaines demanded. He hoped Fanstow had spotted one in a wagon train coming in. It had been a dull period. The boys needed a little activity to restimulate them.

"On that dude Edwards brought in with him," Fanstow said triumphantly.

Gaines snorted. "I guess you're going to walk right into that camp and take it off him."

That stopped the laughter in their faces. Every man here had seen the competent manner in which Edwards' settlers handled those new cap and ball rifles. Those settlers' attention never relaxed for a minute. Edwards saw to that.

Gaines' remark was an affront to Sugg's courage. "I'll walk into that camp anytime I please," he growled.

"Sure," Gaines sneered. This was typical of these men's thinking. They were fortunate they had him to do it for them.

A red glow started in Sugg's eyes. "You just give me a reason," he insisted.

Gaines was weary of the subject. "You fool around that camp, and you'll get your damned head blown off. Has anybody seen Rezin and Haze this morning?"

Shaking heads answered him. He had told Rezin and Haze to report to him this morning. Their indifference was a sign of the way things were slipping. He felt the rage building in him. He'd tighten up things even if he had to shoot a few of them.

Sam Norris came into the room, and excitement showed on his face. If Gaines felt any affection for any man it was this one. Norris was his brother-in-law, and as far as Gaines knew he made a good husband. At least his sister had never complained to him. Norris never questioned a decision Gaines made. They got along fine together.

"Jim," Norris said. "I just come from Edwards' camp. They got Rezin's claybank on their picket line." He licked his lips, and the nostrils of his hatchet nose quivered. He could tell by Gaines' face that he was bringing him news. That always made him feel important. "You know how Rezin feels about that horse."

Gaines knew. He had seen Rezin in desperate need of money and turn down a reasonable offer for the claybank. Now, how did that claybank get in Edwards' camp? It was useless asking Norris. Norris never thought to do a complete job. He'd grab the first scrap of information and run with it.

"Did you see Haze's horse?"

Norris shrugged. "If I did, I couldn't pick it out."

Gaines squinted. It was going to be interesting finding out how Edwards got Rezin's horse. And it might be embarrassing to him. Gaines would enjoy that.

He said softly, "Sugg, you wanted a reason to go into that camp. Find out about the claybank. And take Fanstow with you," he added maliciously. "Maybe he can get that shirt he wants."

Fanstow swallowed nervously. "Just me and Sugg going in?"

"The rest of us will be right there," Gaines soothed him. What he did depended upon how events turned.

40

Talitha slipped away from Chaplin's outstretched arms. "I'm not going to let you go away again," she said. "When you get back you're too—" She searched for the right word.

"Ardent?" Chaplin grinned.

He made a quick grab and caught her wrist. He drew her to him and nibbled at her ear.

"Chichester," she admonished him. "This is awful. Why it's broad daylight."

"You didn't think it was so awful a little while ago."

She was a delight to see when she blushed like that. She had the creamy complexion that took a blush so well. Her hair was the color of ripening wheat straw, and those blue eyes were deep pools beckoning him to drown himself in them.

His lips moved to the base of her throat, and he could feel the increased pound of the pulse there.

"No," she said firmly. "I just know Paw will be after you. I'm surprised he's left us alone this long."

"We're married," he said. "He won't shoot me."

Her eyes were beginning to get that mystic shine that so enthralled him. She might say no, but her eyes belied the word. All he had to do was to apply a little more pressure and that "no" would fade away entirely.

She stirred to a more comfortable position in his arms. "I swear," she said, and her breath fanned his cheek. "If you're not the most persistent man."

She jumped as the voice outside the tent said, "Mr. Chaplin. It's important."

"I knew it," she said forlornly. "Paw's sent for you."

Chaplin swore softly. "Tell him I'll be there in a little while."

"You've got to come now," the voice said. "There's two men at the picket line asking questions about that claybank you brought in. There's another bunch outside the wagons. They look mean. Shall I get Mr. Edwards?"

"Why no," Chaplin drawled. "I'll take care of it myself. I'll be with you in a few minutes, Laughlin."

Talitha watched mournfully as he dressed quickly. She would never completely own this man. Just when she thought she did, something like this happened and pulled him a million miles away from her. He always had that cold, bright look on his face when trouble beckoned.

She asked anxiously, "Chichester, is something wrong?"

He tugged on his boots and picked up his stick. "Nothing's wrong, sugar. I'll be right back."

He bent and kissed her. It was a different kiss, lacking the interest of a few seconds ago.

"Do you know them, Laughlin?" Chaplin asked as he stepped outside the tent.

"I've seen one of them around town," Laughlin said. "He's at least half black with powerful hands." His face was worried. He wished he had gotten Edwards first. But he hadn't quite known what to do. The two men had asked for the man who brought the horse in.

"A mulatto," Chaplin said. Laughlin was right about the power in the man's hands. Chaplin had seen him in the inn one night crush a thick mug to shards with one hand then stand there laughing at the blood flowing from his palm.

Laughlin's face brightened. "There's Mr. Edwards now. I'll tell him—"

Chaplin saw Edwards and Judge Williams sauntering toward the scene. "I'll handle it," he said sharply as he walked to where the horses were tied. Edwards showed no hurry. He looked as though he expected his son-in-law to handle it.

Quite a crowd of people had gathered. Outside the wagons were another half-dozen men. One of them stood in the van, and he looked the part of authority, but Chaplin was sure he belonged to this scum. He would remember the man.

He pushed his way through the crowd and stopped a yard before the dark-skinned man. He put all his attention on him, picking instantly where the menace lay.

"Where'd you get that horse?" The man pointed to the claybank.

It was an insolent question, and Chaplin's

tightening jaws made bony ridges along his cheeks. "That's none of your business, black man." He made "black man" a brutal insult. This man had mixed blood in him. All breeds had blood they wanted to forget.

The man's breathing whistled through his nostrils. His would be a heavy, ponderous rage. It would take him a moment to digest and react to the insult.

The little man said, "Don't let him talk to you like that, Sugg. Break him in two. But don't tear his shirt. I want it." He stretched forth a hand as though he wanted to finger Chaplin's shirt.

Chaplin thrust with the stick. Its point sank deep into the little man's stomach. The air left his lungs in an agonized rush as he bent double. He needed flailing arms to retain his balance, and his arms were doubled across his aching belly. He folded slowly to the ground making queer, gasping sounds.

For an instant Sugg's eyes were round, and his jaw sagged. "Why Goddam you," he roared. "You're going to be powerful sorry about that."

A woman screamed as he sprang forward, his arms extended, his fingers hooked in ugly claws.

A faint, cold smile was on Chaplin's face. He stood rooted until the last split second, then he dipped a shoulder and twisted his body. Sugg couldn't stop his momentum. He threw out a hand in a desperate effort to snag Chaplin's shoulder, and it missed by a fraction of an inch.

The descending stick was a slash of motion. It caught Sugg across the side of the neck. It pulled an animal sound from him, half groan and half grunt. His momentum carried him for a couple of broken steps before his knees unlocked and spilled him.

He twisted back and forth on the ground, and his drawn-back lips displayed the agony in him. A wide, ugly welt was springing into existence along the side of his neck.

Edwards pushed to where Chaplin stood. He looked at the two men on the ground, and his eyes glowed. "I told Judge Williams you wouldn't need any help."

Chaplin looked at Sugg, then at the stick he held. He shook his head and said, "I hit too low. His shoulder took most of it. I meant to break his neck."

He looked at the man with the air of authority standing outside the ring of wagons. "Come and get this scum," he called.

Gaines stared steadily back. He made no sign and uttered no word, but some signal must have passed from him for four men left him and entered the enclosure. Their eyes held awe as they looked at Chaplin, and they gave him wide berth as they assisted Fanstow and Sugg to their feet.

Sugg's head drooped as he leaned heavily on

two men's shoulders. The welt had picked up an ugly, purplish color.

His head raised as he came opposite Chaplin, and pure, naked hating filled his eyes. "You're gonna be sorry about this." His voice was no more than a thin, reedy whisper.

"I am right now," Chaplin answered. "I'm sorry I didn't break your damned neck."

Chaplin saw excited talk break out in the group beyond the wagons. He wasn't close enough to hear what they said. He kept his eyes on the man with the air of authority. There was a sharp intelligence in the man's face. He was a different cut entirely than the rest of them. The rest of them would use a brute force that would be relatively open and easy to answer. But this man had a much greater, potential danger.

He looked up as he felt Chaplin's eyes on him, then turned suddenly and walked away as though disclaiming any connection whatsoever with this bunch.

Chaplin watched him thoughtfully until he was out of sight. He didn't know who the man was, but he was quite certain he would learn soon enough.

Edwards raised his voice to the still-watching crowd. "It's all over. Go on about your business."

They moved slowly away, turning their heads for a final, awed look at Chaplin.

"Hardy enough?" Edwards asked and grinned at Judge Williams.

"More than enough," Williams answered soberly.

That must be some private joke between them for Chaplin didn't understand it at all.

He said fretfully, "I should have killed him." He thought there was shock in the Judge's eyes, and he explained, "Did you see his eyes? I'm going to have to do it one day anyway."

CHAPTER FIVE

The confinement of the camp was becoming galling, and the people were getting restless. Edwards' steps were constantly harassed by settlers demanding to know when they would get their land. Plowmen's hands itched to turn the earth, to prepare it for the spring planting.

Edwards' replies became more and more waspish. "I'm doing everything I can," he'd yell. "Chichester's out surveying every day. And we're rushing the building of the Administration House. I will not be rushed into taking an uncertain step. You're all on a list. Each man will get his land when it comes his turn."

It stopped their grumbling for a day. Tomorrow it would start afresh. Edwards could understand their impatience, but he was moving as fast as was humanly possible.

He stalked toward Chichester's tent at the close of the day. Very few people hailed him, and it angered him. What he did was for their own good, and they couldn't see it. He wasn't going to throw this land open to them and watch the wild scramble that followed. There would be arguments and fights over sites, and he wouldn't have it. Each family on the list would be assigned a piece of land when it came their turn. It would be an orderly, civilized process, and he wasn't going to be pushed into wasteful haste.

Chaplin sat before his tent flaking the dried mud off his boots with the point of a knife. He gave Edwards a brief smile and called, "Talitha, your Paw's here. Set out another stool."

Talitha set out a stool, and her face was reserved as she said, "Hellow, Paw." She wasn't happy with her father. At the rate he was moving she and Chichester would spend the rest of their lives in this tent. She was sure she heard the snickering of kids outside the tent wall last night. She blushed at the thought.

Edwards gave her a heavy nod and dropped on the stool. "Even she's unhappy with me," he said mournfully.

Chaplin pried another flake of mud loose. "A woman hankers after a permanent house."

Edwards gave him a resentful glance. "You think I'm moving too slow?"

"I'm not saying about that. But I know me and my men have laid out a lot of *sitios*. We laid them out real nice with all the lines running square regardless of the land." He added cautiously, "Maybe making a few people happy will hold the rest. At least they'll see some progress."

He knew the famous Edwards temper. It exploded easily at opposition. He waited for Edwards' roar.

Edwards sat in heavy silence staring at the ground. He looked tired and old and defeated. Finally, he spoke. "I wanted the Administration House finished. I wanted all the land surveyed so that everybody could move at once. But maybe you're right."

Chaplin's sigh was inaudible.

"I want you to help me make a sign announcing that people can apply for their land," Edwards said. "I'll hang it in the morning."

Chaplin's grin was a furtive ghost. Maybe he was learning how to handle the old man.

He lettered the sign for Edwards, and he couldn't make Edwards soften it. It announced that people could apply to Edwards for their land. People already occupying land had to prove their right to it at once. If they had no legal title he would throw them off.

The sign was direct. It left a man in no doubt as to where he stood. Right at the beginning it was going to align every squatter against them.

Chaplin said so, and Edwards stared challengingly at him. "Does that worry you?"

The affront showed in Chaplin's eyes. He said

flatly, "We've got enough problems on our hands without making more. We could let the legality of squatters' titles go until we've got our people settled."

Edwards' jaw hardened. "I want that sign hung just as it is."

He stood and walked away. Chaplin's sigh had a different quality. He had congratulated himself prematurely upon learning how to handle the old man.

Chaplin nailed the sign to the live oak tree before Stone House. Stone House stood in the center of the town. It was roofless and windowless, showing the effects of past raids and wars. But its walls were still solid and formidable. He stepped back to where Edwards stood and watched the first man approach the sign.

The man stared at it and scowled. His attitude said he couldn't read it. There would be many of those kind, but there would be more than enough who could read. By nightfall everybody in and around Nacogdoches would know just where Edwards stood.

Another man joined the first one before the sign. He could read, and Chaplin saw his lips move as he read to his companion. He heard their oaths and saw the black anger wash their faces.

He watched through most of the morning, and the reaction was always the same—the oaths and the black anger. Edwards had used a big spoon this time in stirring up trouble.

A crowd was always gathered before Edwards' sign during most of the morning. It changed often but as men drifted away others filled their places. The ground at their boots became muddy as they chewed and discussed this new development. Edwards should have heard some of the names they called him. Chaplin grinned bleakly. It wouldn't bother him at all.

José Sepulveda whittled long splinters from the edge of the fine mahogany table. It was one of a dozen incongruous items of furniture in the one-room log cabin that served as house and office. The structure was set flush with the dirt sidewalk, and one watched his step as he entered, or the resultant jar of stepping down to the earthen floor would rattle his teeth. The place reeked from the rancid smell of old skillet grease thrown on the floor to keep the dust settled. Spread over the uneven surface of the floor were some surprisingly fine pieces of furniture. Some families had never gotten their heirlooms across the Twilight Zone. A beautiful open cabinet filled with excellent china sat against the wall. It was covered with dust and dirt that constantly leaked down from the sod roof. The mahogany table was desecrated by many knife scars, cigarette burns, and the splashing of tallow. Two candles sat on it anchored in the ever-widening base of their melting.

José Sepulveda was proud of his title. He was *alcalde* of Nacogdoches, an office of much dignity and no little responsibility. He glanced at Luis Procela. Procela was just finishing the last of the bottle of whisky. *Madre de Dios*! Procela could drink more whisky than any man he knew. Sepulveda had a fondness for this man. Hadn't both of them suffered much together? They had escaped a United States prison and made their way to the Twilight Zone. He shuddered at the memory. The gringos ran very tough prisons, and their penalties were severe. They had arrived in Nacogdoches to find that Procela's father had just been killed. The son had inherited the office of *alcalde.* Sepulveda had never understood why Luis had been willing to give up a job of so much importance. Luis had shrugged and said, "There are too many papers to read, and I cannot read. You be the *alcalde*, and I will help you."

It was a lazy, comfortable life, but it was vanishing. Sepulveda swore under his breath. Each day added its crushing burden of worry. It all started with the coming of the Americanos. Not Americanos like Captain Jim Gaines, for he had been here long enough to know the problems of how hard life could be in this land—unless a man helped himself to goods he needed to make life more comfortable. It was Americanos like Haden

Edwards who were making life miserable, Americanos who shouted of law and punishment. Sepulveda wanted no more of either.

"I would not be you," Luis Procela said. He squinted into the empty bottle, sighed mournfully, then threw it against the far wall.

Sepulveda sighed. Luis was content to live like a pig. Some day they would have to sweep up and throw out all those broken bottles.

"Why wouldn't you be me?" He had thought he had kept his worry well concealed. Surely, Procela could not have guessed of it.

"You are caught between two Americanos, and you must turn one way or the other. And when you do the other will crush you." He placed his thumb against his palm and ground it, then blew the spot off into nothing. "I will mourn for my friend José Sepulveda."

"The whisky talks," Sepulveda said with great dignity.

"You think so?" Procela's eyes were bright with malice. "You have not read Señor Edwards' sign."

"You talk of reading," Sepulveda jeered.

The pointing out of his lack was no affront. Procela said, "It was read to me. I know what it says."

"And what does it say?" Sepulveda growled.

"It says there is no longer place for men like you and me. That the good life is over. From now on whatever we get we must work for it."

Sepulveda thought the translation came close enough. "The Señor Edwards has no authority over me," he announced.

"Hah," Procela said. "He will take everything from you. Even this miserable cabin. You have no title to it."

He was certain his words were true for there was a fear in Sepulveda's eyes. He knew how to increase the fear. "The *èmpresarios* come, and they mean business," he said. "You have heard what Señor Austin did to Juan Mendoza. He cut off his head and put it on a pole for all criminals to see. No, I would not want to be you."

Sepulveda could think of only one comment. "*Mierda*," he said sourly.

Procela laughed with great delight. "And the *èmpresarios* will have you standing in it right up to your neck."

"Señor Gaines will have something to say about that."

"Ah, you have made your choice," Procela murmured. He waved his hand at the stolen contents in the room. "With all this behind you you can go no other way. Pray you have made the right choice. Pray—"

The door opened cutting off the remainder of his words.

Gaines stepped down into the room, and Norris followed him. Gaines had a somber, brooding look on his face.

It frightened Sepulveda. Yes, the happy days were gone.

"Get out some whisky," Gaines ordered. "And don't tell me you're out. You always got some stashed away."

Sepulveda's face was unhappy as he dug out a bottle from under the eaves. His supply was running low. He hoped Gaines would go on another raid soon and replenish it. He managed a faint grin at the indignant blaze in Procela's eyes. He had let Procela think he was out.

Norris reached for the bottle, and Gaines snatched it out of his hand. His Adam's apple bobbed several times, and the bottle was considerably lighter.

Sepulveda didn't ask if Gaines had read Edwards' sign. When Gaines was in this mood it was best not to speak too many words.

"Norris and me just got into town," Gaines said. "Light those damned candles. A man can't hardly see in this hole."

He took another pull at the bottle before he handed it to Norris.

He pointed an abrupt finger at Sepulveda. "Have you read that goddamned sign?"

Sepulveda uttered a cautious "*Si.*"

"What are you going to do about it?"

Sepulveda threw out his hands in a helpless gesture. "What can I do? I think he has the authority to do as he pleases."

"The hell he has," Gaines roared. "His contract don't say he can throw people off their land and sell it."

"If they have no title—" The scowl on Gaines' face stopped Sepulveda's weak voice.

Gaines glared at Norris and snatched the bottle from his hand. Norris had taken advantage of the time Gaines talked to Sepulveda.

Gaines took a long pull and wiped the whisky from his chin. He grinned maliciously at Norris as he handed the bottle to Procela. Procela's soft sigh was audible to all of them.

"There must be a million titles around here since the Spaniards first took over," Gaines said. "You got the records, José. Get them out."

Sepulveda stood and walked to the old rawhide chest. He opened it and carried several volumes of records back to the table. Much of the paper inside them was brittle and yellowing.

"Get busy, Sam," Gaines ordered. Sepulveda would never be able to read that fine Spanish script.

Norris sat down and opened the first volume. Slowly, he turned page after page. Gaines watched him with infinite patience on his face.

Norris went through several volumes. "Not a million, Jim," he said finally. "But there must be a thousand titles started. Most of them were never proved up. The people who applied for them either were killed or moved on. The only titles that looks to be worth a damn belongs to the Catholic Church and Ellis Bean. Edwards can settle his families just about anywhere he wants."

The relief in Sepulveda's eyes faded as Gaines said, "He can like hell. I expected Bean's title to be good. He got it straight from the Mexican government. All we have to do is to fix these old titles up. We'll write out new ones where we have to, and José will swear to them." He put glittering eyes on Sepulveda. "You'll do that, José, won't you?"

As *alcalde* Sepulveda had the power of a mayor and justice of the peace combined. No one could question him. Nacogdoches had no *ayuntamiento*, or city council, to stop him.

"But that would be—" He fumbled for the word he wanted in English.

"Forgery?" Gaines snorted. "That'd stop you after what you've done?" He stood and came around the table. He placed a hand on Sepulveda's shoulder, and the fingers bit deep. "You're not going to cause me any trouble, are you, José?"

Sepulveda shivered inwardly. The titles Gaines wanted would focus Edwards' attention on him. What would Edwards do to him if he ever found out? It was a terrible question to be asked a man. But Gaines was here. The immediate choice wasn't hard to make.

"I do as you say," he said and sighed.

Gaines' good humor returned. "I thought you

would. I've spent twelve years getting my land together. I knew you wouldn't want me to lose any of it. I'll need a batch of titles. And fix up a lot more for the boys."

Sepulveda's face was miserable. He took all the risks with no profits. "Everyone gains something but me."

Gaines roared with delight. "It's the crime without profit that's bothering you, isn't it, José? We'll make some money out of this. Edwards plans to charge twelve cents an acre. We'll save the boys some money. We'll only charge them ten cents an acre for their titles. Did I ever cut you out of your share?"

Sepulveda's face brightened. His worry had been useless. He should have known that Gaines would come up with an answer to that sign.

"And get a letter off to Saucedo in San Antonio tonight," Gaines said. "Tell him Edwards is throwing Mexicans off their lawful land. He'll believe it coming from you. That'll burn him but good."

The admiration in Sepulveda's eyes grew. Gaines thought of everything. Don José Antonio Saucedo was the political chief of Texas under Don Victor Blanco, governor of Coahuila y Texas. But Blanco maintained his office in Saltillo four hundred miles south of San Antonio. Saucedo had the immediate decisions to make. He was an idealist who wanted to see his people's lot improved. He had been enthusiastically in favor of the Americans coming. Now this would shake him. Yes the Captain Gaines was one smart man.

"Get those titles out in a hurry, José," Gaines ordered. "I hear Edwards is going to organize some Regulators to help him control things. Sam and me are going to offer our help."

Sepulveda's eyes were round. "You would help him?"

Disgust was plain on Gaines' face. "You've got cotton for brains. If we pick the men for his army who's going to control things?"

A great light burst in Sepulveda's face. Yes, he had made the right choice.

Norris' bellow of rage turned his head. "Look at him. He drank every goddamned drop."

Procela hiccupped pleasantly and beamed at them. He held up the empty bottle, then threw it against the far wall. "*Si*," he agreed happily. "While you make the much talk Luis Procela is busy."

CHAPTER SIX

The smell of newness permeated the Administration House. It had a raw, unpainted look and lacked many finishing touches, but it was usable. Edwards had moved in yesterday. He was proud of the building. It was the most elegant structure

59

in Nacogdoches and only the forerunner of many others. Besides its elegance it had another air, an air of permanency, something that had been long missing from any other building in town. It announced to the world that Haden Edwards was here to stay.

He looked up as Chaplin stomped into his office. It was rare that Chaplin ever grew angry enough for it to show openly on his face. Usually, the fire was only in his eyes but this afternoon it covered all his features.

He threw a piece of paper onto the desk. "Here's another title to add to your collection. Every time I finish staking out a piece of land one of these toughs shows up to claim it. How come they never claim any of the unstaked ground?"

Edwards grinned. "What did you do to the claimant?"

"I took his damned title away from him and threw him off."

"Good," Edwards said brusquely. "That's the way I would've handled it."

He opened a desk drawer and pulled out a sheaf of papers. He added Chaplin's title to the pile, then fanned them out across the desk top. "Look at them," he growled. "Titles supposed to be a hundred years old and written on the handmade paper I brought with me from Louisiana. I told you a batch of it was stolen a week ago. I wondered at the time what they wanted it for, then just figured they'd steal anything that wasn't nailed down."

"Forgeries," Chaplin said.

"Every damned one of them. Who's behind it?"

"All of them."

Edwards shook his head. "The bulk of them haven't that much intelligence. No, this came out of one man's fertile imagination."

"Sepulveda?"

"I considered him. I don't think so. Somebody's using his office. I'll find out who it is. In the meantime keep throwing them off."

"It'll be a pleasure," Chaplin assured him.

"We're losing a family in the morning." Edwards laughed at the concern in Chaplin's eyes. "We're losing them the right way. The O'Roarks are moving into their new house in the morning."

The O'Roarks were the first on the list, and Chaplin knew the entire camp had pitched in and helped them build. His surveying duties had kept him so busy he hadn't been able to participate. But the building had started only a few days ago. "I didn't think it'd be finished so soon," he said.

"It's not finished, but it's livable. Seeing them move onto their land will be a tonic for everybody in camp. One thing bothers me though."

"What?" Chaplin asked.

"They'll be three miles from town and all by

themselves. I think it's time to organize a protective force. I've been thinking of what to call it. How does Regulators sound to you?"

Chaplin grinned. "It sounds official and tough. I'll get on it today."

Edwards shook his head. "You haven't the time, and neither do I. I want to move these families out in a hurry. Do you know how many came in the last week?"

Chaplin knew. Twenty-five additional families swelled the camp's population. Something had to be done to move them out.

But whoever led the Regulators had power and responsibility. Edwards had to be careful in picking his man. "Who did you have in mind?"

"A Captain James Gaines," Edwards answered. "He was in to see me yesterday. Do you know him?"

Chaplin shook his head.

"He's the biggest land owner around here. Holds an old Spanish grant. He's several cuts above any of this scum, and he's had military service. He's as interested as you and I in law and order."

Chaplin said dryly, "You got sold on him in a hurry. Have you examined his land titles yet?"

Edwards bristled. "I think I'm a pretty good judge of character. He'll bring in his titles the next time he's in town."

"Sure." That was disbelief in Chaplin's tone.

Edwards pounded his desk. "Goddammit,

Chichester," he roared. "Are you questioning my judgment?"

Chaplin said stubbornly, "I'm just saying that anybody who's living here is liable to be contaminated. I wouldn't trust any one of them as far as I can see them."

Edwards' face was getting that purplish hue it always did when he was crossed.

"But you're the boss," Chaplin said. "You're doing the picking."

Edwards said acidly, "I'm relieved to hear you acknowledge that. Haven't you got something to do?"

Chaplin grinned faintly as he left the office. He had riled the old man considerably. He knew the multitude of problems that beset Edwards. But he shouldn't let the pressure of them push him into a single, hasty step. That was all he was trying to say.

One would have thought the O'Roarks were leaving the country instead of moving just three miles away. Women cried and hugged each other, and men shook hands over and over. O'Roark climbed up on his wagon and lifted the reins. He was a red-faced Irishman, and he waited impatiently while his wife seized another pair of hands.

"Hell, Martha," he said impatiently. "They're all following us out. Will you climb up here so we can get going?"

"Oh, the children," she cried. "I've got to find them."

"They're in the back of the wagon." O'Roark grabbed her extended hand and pulled her into the wagon box. She sat there waving and calling, and he said in disgust, "Oh good Lord."

Most of the camp did troop after them, and each family brought some little gift for the house warming.

Chaplin stood beside Talitha, his arm about her waist. "The O'Roarks are lucky," he commented.

She flashed him a glance. "Why?"

"Because they're the first to move. It's an occasion, and everyone brings gifts. She won't have to cook, and he won't have to work for a year. By the time we build and move it'll be old stuff. Nobody will bring us gifts."

"Oh you," she said in exasperation. This was a sentimental occasion, and he joked about it.

Talitha looked back as they rode away. "At first I envied them moving into their own home and not having to live in a noisy, crowded camp. Now I don't know. That cabin looks so lonely."

That was Chaplin's feeling. He had the impression a mistake was being made, and he couldn't shake it. He reached over and drew her closer to him on the wagon seat.

"I think O'Roark's pretty lucky. He's got her all by herself tonight. Nobody can interrupt him."

"You get worse instead of improving," she said

severely. "Sometimes I believe that's all you think about."

"Do you know anything better to think about?" he drawled.

"What am I going to do with you?" she wailed. She struggled against his restraining arm but not too hard.

He laughed as he saw the dancing sparkle in her eyes and the lovely, slow red creeping into her face.

"It looks to me like somebody else does a little thinking too," he said.

"Chichester!" The impatient voice cut through the fog of his slumber. Talitha stirred on his arm but didn't open her eyes. The day was young for the light filling the tent was weak.

"Coming," he answered in a low voice.

He withdrew his arm from under her head and padded to the tent flap.

"Get dressed," Edwards said. "Don't wake Talitha." His face had a grayness, but the weak light wasn't the cause. This grayness was caused by an inner sickness.

Chaplin dressed and joined him outside the tent.

"It's the O'Roarks," Edwards said, and the sickness was in his voice too. "They were murdered last night and their cabin burned."

The words were a giant fist smashing into Chaplin's stomach and knocking all the air out of him. "Ah no," was all he could say.

Edwards nodded miserably. "Stevens saw smoke a half-hour ago and rode out there. He just reported back."

A dozen men were saddling horses, and Edwards said bitterly, "I'm moving too late. We're going out there now, and there's nothing we can do."

Chaplin's hand rested on Edwards' arm for a moment. Edwards would flog himself with this memory for a long time.

They found a grim scene at the O'Roarks' cabin. The logs were green and hadn't burned well. But the interior was thoroughly gutted. Four charred, scalped bodies were inside the cabin.

The men stood and looked at them, and the sickness was in all their faces as they contrasted yesterday's happy hours with this.

"Damnit," Chaplin raged. "We've got work to do. We can't stand around here with long faces."

He walked to the horses and unstrapped several shovels. He came back and threw them at the men retaining one for himself. He was filled with a helpless rage, a rage that needed a focal point.

They were covering the graves when Gaines rode up. He swung down and approached Edwards. "A sad business, Mr. Edwards. I'm sorry I didn't hear about it sooner."

Edwards nodded heavily. He dropped his shovel and brushed off his hands. "Chichester, this is the man I was telling you about. This is Captain Jim Gaines."

"How did you hear about it?" Chaplin asked. He didn't seem to see Gaines' extended hand.

"Why it's all over town. The scalping says it's Indian work. The Cherokees are getting restless. And I hear the Carancahuas have been putting on war paint."

Chaplin's face seemed swollen with some suppressed feeling. "How did you know they were scalped? They were buried by the time you got here. It isn't even known through our own camp, and yet he says it's all over town. Don't you recognize him?" he shouted at Edwards. "He was with them the morning they came to ask about Rezin's horse. I saw him standing outside the wagons."

The flicker in Gaines' eyes was so brief that no one could swear they had seen it. His laugh sounded easy and true. "You have a good memory, young man. I was strolling by and saw the disturbance. I was fascinated by the way you handled the big mulatto."

"Call him by name," Chaplin said. "You know it."

"Chichester," Edwards thundered.

That dogged stubbornness firmed Chaplin's face. "He's lived here too long and gotten along too well with them. And you're talking about turning your police force over to him. This sad business as he calls it could be a damned good way to make you hurry your decision."

Edwards' jaw sagged. "Are you accusing him of this?"

Gaines said easily, "Don't blame him, Mr. Edwards. Anybody's upset the first time they see the results of an Indian outrage."

Chaplin stared at him. The man was too magnanimous, too forgiving. He said, "Mister, I don't know what you're after, but it smells to me. Before I'd trust you as far as I could see you I'd want to know more about you."

Edwards was red-necked, and his voice was stiff. "That'll do," he said coldly. "I was making my own decisions while you were still wetting your pants."

"Then you haven't learned a hell of a lot," Chaplin said savagely and strode toward his horse. He mounted and looked back. Edwards and Gaines were engaged in earnest conversation. He wondered if Edwards were making more apologies for him.

He rode into camp and put his horse on the picket line. He entered his tent, and Talitha was still sleeping. He shook her gently, and those blue eyes opened.

"You left awfully early this morning," she murmured drowsily. "When I awakened you were gone. I must have gone back to sleep."

She saw the expression on his face, and her eyes cleared. "What is it, Chichester? Paw—"

He wrapped his arms tightly about her. "He's all right, Talitha." In a few more minutes the news would be all over camp. He didn't want her hearing it from somebody else.

"The O'Roarks were murdered last night, Talitha. All of them. Some people claim it was Indian work."

For a long, agonized moment her face was frozen in shock, then it collapsed into tears. He held her tightly and let her cry it out.

"Poor Martha," she said, and he was afraid the tears would begin anew. "This awful land," she wailed.

"Not the land," he said harshly. "Some of the people in it. And your father is a blind fool."

Her eyes widened. "You've had an argument with him."

His eyes smoldered. "Yes. Talitha, how would you like to go back to Louisiana?"

She pulled back so that she could see his face. "You don't mean that, Chichester. You believed in what Paw was doing. He was going to give us land, all the land we wanted. Is that all gone, Chichester?"

"I don't know," he answered wearily. "I just know he's making a mistake. And I can't talk to him about it."

"You've got to try," she insisted. "You can't just ride off and leave him. He needs you."

His pride still smarted at Edwards' siding with an unknown. A question bulked big in his head, and he had to know its answer.

"Will you go with me if I decide to leave?"

She said quietly, "You know I would."

He pulled her to him and kissed her long and hard.

When he released her she asked, "Do you want me to start packing?"

"Not until I have a talk with that old bull head," he growled.

He looked at her with a grave face. "Do you know how much I lean on you, how much I need you?"

"No more than I need you." She opened her arms wide, and the invitation was in the sparkle of her eyes.

"It's broad daylight," he said, and a smile softened his mouth.

"Who cares?" she sniffed.

CHAPTER SEVEN

Chaplin made no attempt to see Edwards until late in the afternoon. He had been busy with a little work of his own, work that he was quite sure Edwards would not approve.

A slow rain was beginning to fall, and Chaplin smiled bleakly. The men who had agreed to ride with him tonight wouldn't be happy about this rain. The moisture from past rains was very near the surface. It took only a slight wetting to bring it back on top. Already the mud in the street was beginning to hold a man's steps.

He stopped in at Elisha Roberts' General Store, the only decent store in town. Roberts had done wonders with this sad wreck of a building. He had patched the roof and whitewashed the walls. The stock of goods he had brought with him was displayed in orderly array. Roberts was luckier than most of the men in camp. He didn't want nor need land. All he needed was a vacant store and a few counters and tables. He had scoffed at Edwards' warning about leaving camp.

"Hell, Haden, I'm setting up a store right in the middle of town. Do you expect these freebooters as you call them to attack me there? Besides I have a hunch these people will be glad to have a store where they can buy something for a change."

His hunch had been right. From the moment he opened his doors he was a success. He was a pleasant-faced man with an efficient, brisk manner. He was the kind of man Edwards saw in his vision of Nacogdoches' streets lined with prosperous stores.

He smiled as Chaplin entered. He liked Edwards' son-in-law though he thought his garb foolish in this country. Particularly on a day like this. Those elegant trousers were picking up quite a few mud spots. Did Chichester wear these clothes to deliberately provoke these people or was he just a little ahead of his time? It was an interesting question, and someday Roberts might see the answer unfold.

"Hello, Chichester," he said, "how are things going?"

Chaplin's expression was gloomy. "Bad right now. You heard about the O'Roarks."

Roberts' face sobered as he nodded. "A bad business, Chichester."

"It could be even worse than that," Chaplin said grimly. "Elisha, how well do you know this man Gaines?"

"I know him by sight. He's been in a few times, and he seems pleasant enough."

"Is he one of them?"

Roberts knew what Chaplin meant by the ambiguous question, and his eyes narrowed as he considered it. "I don't know," he answered finally. "I've seen some of the known freebooters with him." He saw the triumphant flash in Chaplin's eyes and cautioned, "But he lives here. He'd have to be friendly with them to a degree to be able to live here. Why?" he asked with normal curiosity.

"Haden and I argued about him," Chaplin said. "I say he's putting too much trust in him."

Evidently, the clash had scraped Chaplin raw. Roberts was surprised it hadn't come sooner. Both of them were strong-willed men as tough in their own way as any freebooter in Nacogdoches.

"Thanks, Elisha," Chaplin said and turned to leave. His eye caught a display of hand mirrors on a table. They should delight any woman's heart. They were long-handled and fashioned daintily.

The handle and casing were mother-of-pearl, and the soft colors wove intricate designs with each other.

Roberts laughed at the picture of Chaplin looking at himself in the mirror. "One of them should come in now and see you holding that, Chichester. You'd be done."

Chaplin grinned. "It could get me in trouble, couldn't it. I was thinking of one for Talitha."

"She'd love it," Roberts assured him. "I'm going to camp in a little while, I'll take it to her."

Chaplin paid him and said, "Tell her it's from an unknown admirer."

He walked out and stood for a moment in reflection. He hadn't picked up anything definite. What Roberts said about Gaines could be true—that the man had to associate with the toughs because he lived here. But wasn't a man judged by the company he kept?

He sighed and turned toward the Administration House. He couldn't put off facing the old man any longer.

He walked into the office, and Edwards raised his head. There was a pathetic eagerness in his eyes as he greeted him.

"Talitha all right?" he asked gruffly. What he was actually asking was, Is everything all right between us?

"Fine," Chaplin said in a noncommittal voice.

Both of them were skirting this morning's incident.

Edwards brought it out into the open. "Gaines is bringing in his titles tomorrow." An edge was in his voice. That should be proof enough to Chaplin. An honest man would want his titles examined.

"Good," Chaplin answered, and the word had no giving in it.

He heard yelling in the street and moved to the window.

A troop of horsemen were massing, and they yelled at and cursed each other good naturedly.

Edwards joined Chaplin at the window. "The man's been busy today. That's the second patrol he's organized. He took the first one out himself about an hour ago. He thinks he can run down the Indians that attacked the O'Roarks."

Chaplin held the caustic comment he wanted to make. There were some twenty-five men in that bunch, and not one of Edwards' settlers was among them. Gaines probably led a patrol of equal size. That would be fifty men. Chaplin would bet that nobody could find fifty honest men living around here.

They were a motley, dirty crew dressed in every conceivable garb. They looked just like the men who frequented the inn, the men who loitered on the street corners. They wore a common label, and anybody but a blind man could see it.

He murmured, "I'm not sure I'd want that bunch protecting me."

Edwards flared. "Goddammit, Chichester. You can't expect them to be dressed in neat uniforms. What can we lose? They're doing it on a voluntary basis." His face turned red at Chaplin's expression. "I'm keeping an eye on them."

"I would," Chaplin said dryly.

The horsemen lined out in the street and passed the window. One of them turned his face toward it. His face was horribly pocked by the ravages of smallpox. He saw the two men in the window and thumbed his nose at them.

"You've got a real respectful army, General," Chaplin drawled.

Edwards' face could turn the most amazing shade of red. Chaplin left the office before he watched Edwards choke to death.

This morning's argument still yawned between them. A few more words, and both of them would step back into it over their heads.

He was glad he hadn't told Edwards what he had in mind, or the old man would have canceled it. When Edwards set his mind trying to change it was like a breeze trying to nudge a giant oak.

Before I'm through I'll rub his nose in it, Chaplin vowed, and there was malice in the thought.

He went back to camp and collected the dozen

men he had selected. None of them was happy at the prospects of a night's ride in this rain. But Chaplin had a definite goal now. He wanted to cut the trail of either of Gaines' patrols; he wanted to see what those patrols were actually doing.

He stared coldly at the grumbling men and said, "That could've been your family out there this morning."

That left guilty looks on their faces, and it stilled the grumbling.

Chaplin mounted and led them out. Talitha wasn't very happy about him going. She hadn't expressed it in so many words, but it had been in her eyes. He thought with grim amusement, everybody's unhappy tonight.

The night enveloped them in a thick, black, wet blanket. Vision was limited to a few feet. The rain lessened to a steady drizzle, and Chaplin listened to the suck of the hoofs being pulled out of the mud. There wasn't much else to listen to. About midnight he admitted the apparent uselessness of this nocturnal ride. They couldn't see, and there was nothing to hear but the pull of hoofs from the clinging earth. But he kept doggedly on casting his circle about Nacogdoches ever larger. Somewhere out in this black night fifty men were riding, and he had to cut some sight or sound of them. A jeering thought flashed into his mind. They could be holed up somewhere in the dry. After making a big show to impress Edwards they could now be sitting under a roof laughing at him.

Stevens said, "Chichester, we're not doing any good."

It didn't take much astuteness to make that observation, Chaplin thought irritably. Still he couldn't keep them riding around much longer without some tangible results.

He said, "A few minutes longer. Keep your eyes open for something like a flash of light." He hoped they would spot light from a struck match or the winking, red eye of a sucked-on cigarette. He admitted how forlorn the hope was.

He was ready to give the order to turn back when he thought he caught something ahead. It wasn't exactly a light but more of a lessening of the darkness ahead.

They rode steadily in that direction, and he saw the orange glow creep up from the earth and push against the night's blackness.

Several of them saw it at the same time, and he heard the outbreak of their excited cries.

"It looks like a fire," he said. "A big one." The Sabine River should be just ahead. "Probably coming from this side of the river."

In the time it took to say those few words the orange hue was changing to a deeper red. It would take a large fire to make that much light.

"Move up easy," he cautioned.

He halted them two hundred yards from the fire. At least six wagons had been run together in a pile and set fire to. The flames crackled lustily despite the dampness of the night.

He stared at the scene somber-faced. He felt sure whoever was responsible for this had gone. The fire illuminated a large radius, and he could see the sprawled forms of a dozen people.

"Cover me," he said. "I'm going in."

He rode to where the heat of the fire halted him. Yes there had been six wagons in the train, and all of its occupants were murdered. A sneak attack under the cover of the wet night with these people dead before they knew what was happening. He turned in the saddle, waved his arm, and his men joined him.

The skies opened, and the rain pelted in a deluge. The flames fought back spitting like an enraged cat, but they fought a losing battle. They subsided sullenly hissing under the dousing.

One of the men saw a barrel some fifty feet from the rear of the ruins of a wagon. He walked to it and examined its broached head.

"Chichester," he called. "Come here."

Chaplin joined him, and the whisky smell was strong. The barrel was empty, but the black, three-inch letters on its side said this had been a barrel of Monongahela whisky.

The man asked, "I wonder if this was the only one?"

Chaplin shrugged. If there were more they had been carried away. Why couldn't he have been just a little earlier? Why couldn't he have caught them as they were broaching this barrel?

He said with weary rage, "There's nothing we can do here tonight. We'll send a party back in the morning." These people had come to Texas with the bright promise of cheap land luring them. The promise was as dead as the soaked ashes.

They were a depressed bunch of men as they rode away. Stevens asked, "Do you think it was Indians, Chichester?"

"Maybe," he said harshly. And maybe not. There had been fifty men wandering around in this rain-soaked night. The vain regret came back to him. Why couldn't he have been just a little earlier? Instead of returning emptyhanded he knew he would be bringing some proof back to Edwards.

Edwards had left the camp by the time Chaplin awakened in the morning. He refused Talitha's offer of breakfast and said, "I've got to see your Paw."

"Is it more trouble?" she asked.

"What gave you that idea?" His tone was irritable.

"You," she said quietly. "You haven't spoken a half-dozen words, and you should see the way you look."

He kissed her and said, "No trouble." He headed for town remembering the look in her eyes. He hadn't fooled her at all.

He found Edwards just coming out of Roberts' store. Edwards' face was hostile as he said, "I hope you enjoyed your night's ride."

Edwards knew about the start of the ride; he didn't know about the finish for Chaplin doubted any of his men had been up by the time Edwards left camp.

"Not very much," he said soberly. "It's never very pleasant to look at massacred people."

The hostility faded from Edwards' eyes. His voice was jerky as he asked, "What did you find?"

"A six-wagon train wiped out. The raiders got whisky. How much I don't know. We found an empty Monongahela barrel."

Edwards chewed on his lower lip. "What do you think?"

Chaplin's face was cold. "If you want proof I haven't got it. The rain washed out their tracks. I couldn't trail them."

He heard a burst of laughter and turned his head. Six men lurched down the street. If the unsteady walk wasn't enough to tell one they were drunk the glassy shine in their eyes and the vacant expression on their faces should do it. The odd assortment of bottles they carried was only superfluous evidence.

The pock-marked man was with them. He saw Edwards and Chaplin and threw out an arm stopping the others. "Got to pay respects to the general," he said in a slurred voice. "Bes' lil' ole general in whole goddamned country."

He stepped forward and thrust a bottle in Edwards' face.

Edwards' eyes blazed as he knocked the hand aside.

"Hell," the man protested. "Thas good Monongahela whisky. We got three barrels of it. You can drink all you want."

"You had four, didn't you?" Chaplin asked icily.

"Had four," the man agreed. Something got through to him for an uneasy flicker showed in his eyes. "No three," he said.

"You son-of-a-bitch," Edwards breathed. He stepped forward and hit the man in the face.

It was a good blow. It knocked him down. He stared up at Edwards, and his eyes were bewildered. He asked plaintively, "What did you do that for? I'm one of your Regulators."

The other five surged forward. Chaplin's hands gripped the stick at both ends. He was poised on the balls of his feet, and a bright flame danced in his eyes.

They looked at him, and they looked at Edwards. The fury in his face was an awesome sight. The surge melted into indecisiveness.

"You're not one of my Regulators," Edwards raged. "You tell Gaines and that crooked *alcalde* of his that I'm cleaning up this town. I'm calling for a new election next week. It'll be held December fifteenth. You tell him that."

He lifted his eyes to the five men standing opposite him. "Drag him out of here," he ordered. "I'm sick of looking at you."

A faint grin played on Chaplin's lips as he watched them help the pock-marked man to his feet. His father-in-law didn't need his nose rubbed in fecal matter to identify it. He could smell it as far away as the next man.

"Who are you going to run for *alcalde*?" he asked.

"You."

Chaplin's jaw dropped. "Me?" he spluttered.

"What's the matter?" Edwards asked coldly. "Don't you think you can handle it?"

Chaplin laughed. He was back on firm footing with Haden Edwards. "I can handle it. I was just wondering what Talitha was going to say about it."

CHAPTER EIGHT

Chaplin walked into Edwards' office. It was a bare room filled with the not unpleasant smell of raw lumber. A battered desk and two uncomfortable chairs were the only items of furniture. Its one window looked out onto the town's main street.

As usual Edwards was buried under the press of

paperwork. Chaplin thought, He never knows a relaxed minute. Empire building was no job for a man with languorous tendencies.

He said, "I checked out Ellis Bean's title. It's good." He took a chair and stretched his long legs out before him. "I had a long talk with him. He's got quite a background."

Edwards glanced at him. "I know he holds a suspicious amount of land."

"The Mexican government gave it to him. I've seen enough titles to know a good one."

Edwards grunted in annoyance. Bean, sitting on all that land, was an irritant to him. "You've seen some counterfeit titles too."

His father-in-law could alienate a man with sheer obstinacy. He had hoped to find Bean's titles worthless, and in disappointment he had to question Chaplin's judgment.

Chaplin grinned. "I'd rather have him with us than against us. He's what I'd call one tough man. He's been in Texas since eighteen hundred. He knows it, and he knows Mexican politics."

Edwards' annoyance increased at Chaplin's defense, and he transferred his rancor to Ellis Bean. "I'll treat him no differently than I would the next man. He should have come in and presented his credentials like everybody else."

Chaplin smiled faintly. "He's used to having people come to him. Names don't mean much to Ellis Bean. He's run with the biggest. He fought with Andy Jackson and Jean Lafitte. He's been in two dozen revolutions down in Mexico. I think the Mexican government gave him his land hoping he'd settle down. It seems to be working. Now all he wants to do is to raise a few horses and a little cotton."

He had liked Bean at first sight, recognizing a kindred spirit. They had sat talking for three hours, and one bottle of whisky and part of another had made it a pleasant, fast-passing time.

"He sounds like a troublemaker to me," Edwards said flatly.

Chaplin shook his head. Haden Edwards could turn as obstinate as any mule.

He said softly, "Just don't push on him, Haden. The Mexican government appointed him Indian agent for Texas. They even keep a garrison of twelve soldiers at his Fort Teran. If he gets set against us I think he could hurt us."

Edwards snorted. Chichester had some impressionable ideas.

"Did you see Gaines?" he asked abruptly.

"I couldn't find him."

"Maybe you spent too much time talking to this Bean."

Chaplin said calmly, "I don't think so." He might increase Edwards' annoyance, but he had to tell him one more thing. "I told you Bean knows Mexican politics and politicians. He says Saucedo is a fair man. He thinks it would be smart to keep him informed of every step you take."

Edwards' eyes smoldered. "I informed him I was holding the election. I've got the right. I don't have to waste my time telling him why. I'm not begging Saucedo for anything."

Chaplin sighed. He had taken the wrong tack in playing up Ellis Bean. "How's the election look?" he asked.

"Good. Gaines is running Norris against you. He thinks Norris will pick up all the American votes. He's wrong. The new settlers won't vote for him. And the old ones are beginning to realize that if they want any real security it'll come from me. Not from Gaines. I'm the only one who can give them a legal title to their holdings."

Edwards never recognized an obstacle in his path. His blind optimism could be irritating. Or was it pure stubbornness that refused to let him acknowledge that he could ever be wrong? Chaplin pondered it. Maybe the two traits were compatible. Maybe it was the stubbornness that made the optimism come true.

Edwards said pointedly, "I want you to see Gaines and get a look at his titles."

Chaplin wanted to tell him to feel his way, to take a step at a time instead of bulling his way forward. It would be a waste of words. When Haden Edwards was convinced he was right nothing deterred him.

He said in weary resignation, "As soon as I can find him." He doubted if a word he had said about Bean stuck in Edwards' mind.

"You're not sore about the coming election, are you, José?" Gaines said.

Sepulveda had given it some thought. In some ways he was unhappy about losing his authority. But in other ways it was probably best that he step down. This was a fight between two powerful Americanos, and he had noticed that when Americanos fought other people got hurt. If Señor Norris won there would be very little change in the way of life. But if Señor Chaplin won there would be much change, and he, José Sepulveda, would suffer most.

He smiled and said, "I am not too unhappy."

Gaines whacked him on the back. "That's the spirit. You won't be sorry. Saucedo's got my letter by now. It'll burn him. He won't think Edwards's got the right to throw out the *alcalde* just because he's Mexican."

Alarm flashed in Norris' eyes. "You sound like you think we're going to lose."

"Hell no we're not going to lose. But I don't overlook a thing. I'm going to write Saucedo again just in case something does go wrong. If I see we might lose the election I'll send it to him."

He drew out a piece of paper and poised a pen over it. "Let's see. I'll start out by saying Edwards couldn't stand to obey Mexican law. With his own man in office he can do anything he wants to the poor Mexicans. He ran a crooked election. He brought in every outlaw from the Twilight Zone and voted them."

For a moment the scratching of his pen was the only sound.

He looked up and said, "Come on, come on. I need some ideas."

Norris' face lighted. "He even voted travelers just passing through Nacogdoches."

Gaines grinned. "Sam, I was wrong about you never having a thought."

The pen scratched again.

Sepulveda said timidly, "The poor, loyal Mexicans were crushed by the mountain of crooked votes."

Gaines slapped his thigh. "That's the touch I need, José."

He wrote rapidly, then read aloud, "And I respectfully submit, Don José Antonio Saucedo, that if this election fraud is allowed to stand you can guess how your people will be abused."

Norris said admiringly, "That's it, Jim. Saucedo will choke if he ever gets that letter."

Sepulveda smiled. "Don José will be very unhappy if he thinks his people are abused. It could even bring him storming up here."

Gaines folded the letter carefully. "We wouldn't want him to make that long trip. All we want him to do is to send a letter throwing out the election. José, you put this away someplace and keep it clean. I might have to send it." His eyes sharpened. "José, as outgoing *alcalde* you can act as supervisor of the election."

An uneasy look stole across Sepulveda's face. "What am I supposed to do?"

Gaines' grin had a wolfish cast. "Why, count the votes. That's all."

Sepulveda spread his hands helplessly. "But the counting I do not do so well."

"You can throw out the votes you suspect. And you suspect a lot of them already, don't you? Especially the ones cast for Chaplin. Now tell me what's hard about that?"

Sepulveda gulped. "If Edwards and Chaplin are there it could be very hard."

"But you're going to do it, aren't you, José?"

Sepulveda nodded miserably. "I will do it." He wished this cursed election was over. He would gladly give up this office with its fine furniture and move back to his shed.

Edwards was in an exuberant mood election afternoon. "It's going our way. I can tell."

"I wish I could be as sure," Chaplin drawled.

"Look at those long faces," Edwards said impatiently. He pointed to a group of men standing across the street. "I'd need a yardstick to measure them. They know how it's going."

Chaplin looked thoughtfully at the men. Sam Norris was there whittling on a stick. His strokes were long and vicious, the strokes an upset man makes. Edwards could be right. A lot of men going into Elisha Roberts' store to vote had paused long enough to wish them luck. He hoped their wishes and their voting were on the same plane.

He smiled and said, "It's aroused a lot of feeling anyway. There's been a dozen fights in town this afternoon. Jed Stevens broke a bottle over one of their heads."

Edwards peered at him suspiciously. "Were you in that fight?"

"No," Chaplin said regretfully. "Jed was doing all right. I just sort of kept the others off him."

Edwards grunted. His face was fretful as he looked up and down the street. "I thought Gaines would be in town today. I wanted to talk to him."

Chaplin had looked for him too, but if Gaines had been in town he'd stayed out of sight. "Maybe he'd rather lose his vote than have his titles questioned."

Edwards said darkly, "They're going to be questioned sooner or later. Here comes a vote for them."

Chaplin turned his head. Fanstow, the little man he had punched in the belly with his cane was crossing the street. Edwards was right about that vote being gone.

Fanstow stopped, and his manner was nervous.

Those men across the street seemed to be bothering him a great deal.

"Mr. Edwards, can I talk to you?"

"We got nothing to talk about."

"Every man deserves to have his say," Chaplin drawled. His eyes were keen as he watched the little man.

Fanstow looked at him gratefully. "Mr. Edwards, I thought I had a legal title to my land. I'm not so sure now."

Edwards snorted. "You know goddamned well it's no good."

Fanstow plowed ahead doggedly. "Could I get a legal title from you?"

Chaplin interrupted before Edwards could swear at the man. "How much land do you have?"

"A square league."

Chaplin did some rapid mental calculation. "It'll cost you about five hundred dollars."

Edwards' laugh was harsh. "He never saw that much money."

Fanstow said stubbornly, "I've got it. Can I get a title from you?"

Edwards caught Chaplin's warning glance. "See me in the morning," he said sourly.

He glared at Chaplin as Fanstow went into the store to cast his vote. "I'm not sure I want his kind."

"You said they'd be switching over to you. Turn him down, and the word'll get around."

Edwards nodded a grumpy agreement. He pulled out his watch and looked at it. "Three more hours," he said and sighed.

Chaplin shifted his weight. They had stood here since the polls opened. Edwards' feet must be complaining bitterly about the weight they supported. But the election was going in an orderly manner. No one had tried to vote more than their allotted time, and he hadn't seen anybody who wasn't eligible to vote.

Fanstow came out and nodded brightly to them. He said, "I'll see you in the morning, Mr. Edwards." He looked like a man who after laboring to a decision felt an immense relief.

Edwards nodded coldly, but Chaplin grinned at Fanstow. If the man wanted to settle down he felt no malice.

"I wonder if Gaines is going to try to slip in just before the polls close," Edwards said.

"I think he'll pass it up entirely." Gaines would lose his vote but that was better than facing either of them.

The voting slowed to a trickle after being fairly heavy through the morning hours. Chaplin couldn't see how there could be many eligible voters left.

Edwards kept trying to hurry the closing hour by glancing frequently at his watch. He held it in his hand the last few minutes, then said, "That does it."

He strode toward the door of Roberts' store, and Chaplin followed him.

Roberts met them and asked, "Who's going to clean up my store?" but there was no real protest in his voice.

Chaplin grinned at the muddy path leading from the doorway to the voting table. The other tables, filled with merchandise, had been pushed back to clear an area for the voting.

"Looks like you did a business today, Elisha."

"And never made a dime," Roberts said. His eyes were sparkling. "My main worry was that they'd steal me blind. I think we had us an honest election, Chichester."

"We'll see."

It had been a simple election. The voting was for one office and two men. A voter had merely to scrawl his choice of candidate on a slip of paper and put it into the ballot box. Judge Williams sat behind the table, and his face looked tired. He had been on duty since early in the morning.

"Look at him," Williams said jerking his head toward Sepulveda. "Doesn't his expression tell you something?"

Sepulveda lounged against a far wall. His face was mournful.

Williams laughed. "His face says you've won, Chichester. It looks as though I'll have to treat you with more respect."

"Close the door, Elisha," Edwards ordered.

Sepulveda straightened and took a deep breath. He approached the table and said, "I will take the box, no," and reached for the ballot box.

Edwards struck an extended hand aside. "You will take it, no," he mimicked.

"But I count the votes," Sepulveda protested. He looked uneasily at the stern faces. "I do not count so good unless I am alone."

"You do not count at all unless you count here," Edwards said.

Sepulveda shifted his weight, and his expression was pleading. "But—"

"Throw him out, Chichester."

Chaplin started to move, and Sepulveda flung up a hand. "I count here," he said hastily. Gaines' wrath would be terrible, but what more could he do?

He sat down at the table, and his mind was a rat caught in a trap running against first one wall then another. Could he detract their attention and grab and pocket a handful of votes? But four pairs of stern eyes watched his every move. To do something as he first thought would be suicide.

He unfolded the first slip of paper and stared at it hopelessly. Gaines said throw out the votes he suspected. But on what grounds? He did not even know the man who had written this vote.

He said in a forlorn voice, "Señor Chaplin," and laid the paper on the table.

Williams made a mark on a slip of paper and moved the ballot closer to him.

Sepulveda opened another paper. "Chaplin." He counted twelve votes in a row for Chaplin, and his spirits sank lower and lower. Then he read off three consecutive votes for Norris, and his face brightened.

Williams made two neat piles of the votes. "If we have to recount we won't have to separate the votes again."

Sepulveda sighed. He was saying Chaplin's name again with monotonous frequency.

Before the count was half-completed Sepulveda knew the result. The pile of votes for Señor Chaplin was so much higher than the pile of votes for Señor Norris.

He pushed back from the table and stood. "I think you have won," he said and thrust a limp hand in Chaplin's direction.

Chaplin grinned broadly. "And you are glad, aren't you, José?"

"*Si*, señor," Sepulveda said weakly and shuffled to the door. He looked back for a brief instant. *Dios Mio*, he thought passionately. He had done his best. Señor Gaines could not expect the impossible.

He shivered at the intentness of the Americans' gaze, then stepped outside and closed the door behind him.

Edwards roared with laughter. "I'd like to see

Gaines' face when he tells him." A thought struck him and broke up the laughter. "Chichester, if we follow him he might lead us to Gaines."

Chaplin nodded and crossed the floor after Edwards. By the time they came outside Sepulveda was across the street talking to Norris.

They were too far away to hear the words, but the tight, strained lines of their bodies said they might be arguing. It looked as though Norris was accusing and Sepulveda was trying to defend himself.

Suddenly, Norris turned and strode toward a man waiting beside a saddled horse. He said a few words to the man and handed him something. The man vaulted into the saddle, whipped his mount around and raced out of town.

"He's in a hurry to get the news to Gaines," Edwards said.

Chaplin's face was thoughtful. "My guess is that courier is on his way to San Antonio with a letter for Saucedo. If so Saucedo is going to be reading Gaines' side without hearing yours."

Edwards shrugged. The shrug said, Who cares?

CHAPTER NINE

Norris had a head the following morning. It felt as though it stretched from wall to wall. It wasn't the result of a victory celebration. Maybe he ought to call it a defeat celebration. He had wanted that office. He had been surprised at the intensity of his wanting. But being *alcalde* would have given him a step of his own, one he could stand on all by himself without Gaines edging him off it.

"Just wait until Gaines gets here," he growled. "He's going to peel the hide off of you."

The acrimonious argument had gone on all morning. It had lasted so long that Sepulveda's natural fear of the Americans was dissipated in the rising heat of his emotions.

"I do everything I can," he said hotly. "I do not give the damn what you or Señor Gaines think."

Procela sat in a tipped-back chair against the far wall. Sugg stood near him, and Procela looked at him and shook his head. Sugg knew what Procela meant, and he was in agreement for he nodded in return. But Sugg was like Luis Procela—too wise to try to stop the argument.

Profound pity was on Procela's face as he looked back at Sepulveda. Norris had baited his friend so long that Sepulveda's tongue had thrown its bridle. He had already said an unwise thing. Gaines could bait him into saying more.

Yes, it was time to make the interruption even if it made Sepulveda mad at him. He said softly, "José, the last of the whisky was gone an hour ago. I am very dry."

"There is no more," Sepulveda said angrily.

Procela's tone was mournful. "Then all the

whisky you have hidden will do you no good. When this Chaplin comes to take over your office he will find it."

Sepulveda's nostrils flared. "He will not take my office—until I say he can," he finished weakly.

"Hah," Norris snorted. "He'll throw you out right on your ass."

Sepulveda's voice raised a pitch. "If he comes here we'll throw him out on his ass." He searched Procela's face. "Won't we, Luis?"

Procela's eyes wavered. "It is not my fight," he muttered.

Sepulveda's eyes blazed at him. "But you ask for my whisky," he said bitterly.

Sugg flexed his hands, and there was a hungry eagerness in the motion. "I'll help you, José." His voice came out as a thin, tinny squeak. Ever since Chaplin had hit him with that cane his voice had never been right. Last night he had heard two women at the tavern laughing about his voice. He had thrown aside the curtain of the cubicle in which they were sitting, and they had screamed at the rage in his face. He had wanted to crush them, one in each big hand. He remembered the eagerness in those hands. It had had a live, crawling quality. It was back this morning.

"I wish he would come." It didn't come out the growl he intended. It came out a mousy squeak, and his eyes darted suspiciously from face to face. Nobody had the slightest glimmer of laughter in their eyes. "Maybe he wouldn't be alive to take over José's office."

Norris' face brightened. This might he an answer to the problem, an answer Gaines had never thought of. If Chaplin came here and started a fight could anybody blame them for defending themselves?

"José, count me in," he said. "If it came to a fight you know I'd stand behind you."

Sepulveda gave him an unforgiving glance before he placed a chair at the base of a wall. He stood on the chair and fumbled around deep under the eaves.

Procela's mouth watered as he saw the bottle in Sepulveda's hand. He had searched those eaves. José was very clever when he came to hiding his whisky.

Sepulveda uncorked the bottle and handed it to Sugg. He looked coldly at Norris and Procela. He knew who his friends were. Maybe he would relent. Maybe he would give the two false ones a tiny drink when the bottle was almost empty. He watched in admiration as Sugg's Adam's apple continued to bob. Whisky ran down in a steady little stream from Sugg's lip corner. *Madre de Dios*! He should have brought out two bottles.

Edwards said, "You're crazy, Chichester, to go in after those records alone." Chaplin's face remained stubborn, and Edwards sighed. "You don't have to prove anything to me."

Chaplin looked momentarily startled before he grinned. A dozen men were gathered near Sepulveda's cabin, and there was an eager waiting in their faces.

"Maybe I'm trying to prove something to them. I don't want them thinking they've got a weak *alcalde*."

He was dressed in his best, and except for the mud on his boots and lower trouser legs his clothing was spotless. He used the knob of his cane to tip his hat at a more jaunty angle.

He grinned again before he started across the street. "If I don't come out in a reasonable time, say in a day or two, you'd better send after me."

"You just like trouble," Edwards accused.

Chaplin looked horrified. "Why I run when I hear the word."

He picked his way around the heavier puddles in the street. His face was distressed at the amount of mud he was picking up on his boots. If this miserable weather didn't let up he would spend most of his life polishing his boots.

He rapped sharply on the door of the cabin, then kicked it open. He stood on the high threshold surveying the four men in the room. He knew Norris, Sepulveda, and Sugg. Sugg had just taken a whisky bottle from his mouth. His eyes were reddened and wild. Chaplin didn't know the smaller, shifty-eyed Mexican.

"I've come for the records," he said.

The four looked at him for a long, weighing moment, then glanced at each other. No emotion showed, but there was an agreement in that glance.

"Well you just come and get them," Sugg said.

"I'll do that," Chaplin said brightly.

He left the high threshold in a flying leap, and Sepulveda was the closest. Sugg threw the bottle he held, but his timing was slow. It crashed against the wall just behind Chaplin's head.

Chaplin drove his boot heels into Sepulveda's crotch, and heard the man's alarmed shout break into a sickened gargle. Sepulveda dropped his arms, wrapping them weakly around Chaplin's legs, almost pulling him down. Chaplin flailed his arms to regain balance, and his momentum carried him across the room. He whirled, and Sepulveda lay on the floor moaning and writhing.

The three left on their feet moved in on him in a fan-shaped approach. Chaplin surveyed them with bright, dancing eyes. Norris had picked up a stick of firewood, but even with that advantage Chaplin decided the big mulatto was the more dangerous.

He feinted at the smaller Mexican, then whipped the cane around at Sugg's head. The feint didn't fool Sugg, or maybe he was cane-wise. He jerked his head aside, and instead of the cane crunching against solid bone it just peeled a little scalp.

Missing that blow was bad. Chaplin had put all the savage ferocity he could into it, and the effort left him momentarily unprotected.

Norris threw the stick of firewood, and it slashed across the side of Chaplin's throat. It was a hard blow; it put a gagging sickness in his mouth and watered his vision. He staggered backward trying to firm the muscles in his legs, but it was like trying to walk on string instead of bone.

Norris yelled triumphantly and dived in at Chaplin. The smaller Mexican was coming in from the other side, and Chaplin beat ineffectually at them. Norris' arms were wrapped about him, and the Mexican was twisting him from the other side. Their heads were buried against his body, and his blows slid off their shoulders and backs.

They wrestled him to the floor, and he tried to roll to throw off their weight. He felt the jarring thumps as they drove knees and elbows into him, and fingers clawed at his face.

Sugg danced about the heaving, twisted pile trying to drive a boot into Chaplin's head. Chaplin threw the two men on top of him first one way then the other trying to avoid those kicks. If one of them landed, his head would fly across the room. A boot drove into his shoulder, and he felt his grip on his cane loosen. He had to get on his feet, he had to get his cane arm free. If he could get one good, solid blow he could cut down the odds.

A knee rammed into his stomach sending waves of nausea through him. His mouth was open as he gagged for air, and he almost missed seeing the boot flying at his face. He jerked his head back, and the toe grazed his chin. He felt the fiery burn in the wake of its path, and lights burst before his eyes. He thought in wonder, four of them were too much for me.

A great roaring filled the room, and he had to concentrate to determine where it came from. At first he thought it must be coming from inside his head, then he heard distinct words, and he wasn't saying them.

"Goddam you," Edwards roared. "I said get back." His arm swept out and smashed across Sugg's chest, and the mulatto fell back a step.

It looked as though the wildness in Sugg's eyes wouldn't let him see the pistol, and hope burned in Edwards' eyes.

"Take that step," he begged. "Come on. Take it."

Partial sanity returned to Sugg's eyes, and his face turned sullen. He wiped his mouth with the back of his hand and muttered something, but he stayed where he was.

Edwards kicked Procela off of his son-in-law, and Procela's eyes went round at sight of the pistol. He retreated to a corner and cowered there.

"You need more help?" Edwards asked.

The question enraged Chaplin. He hadn't asked Edwards to come in here. Now his father-in-law was questioning his ability to handle Norris.

Norris' body was pressed against him, and Chaplin couldn't get his knee very high. But the six inches were enough. He rammed it into Norris' groin, and the explosive burst of air was part grunt, part groan. Chaplin rolled one way then the other, and he got force and momentum into his heave. Norris' hands tried to clutch at him, but he was hurting, and the fingers kept slackening. They slid down Chaplin's coat sleeve and fastened again at the cuff. Chaplin's coat gave at the shoulder seam, and the sleeve went with Norris. Norris lay on his back rocking from side to side, his hands holding the ache deep in the pit of his belly.

Chaplin pushed to his feet. His head hung low, and his breathing had a harsh, tearing sound. He could feel the pain begin to nibble at him now, and its teeth would grow. He hadn't been aware of the bruises and lacerations until this brief respite. They couldn't have had him down for more than a few seconds, but they had mauled him good.

He raised his head and looked at Norris, and the rage and pain pulled an unconscious yell from him. He dove at Norris, and his weight smashed Norris against the dirty floor. His hands locked around Norris' throat, and the thumbs dug deeply into the hollow at the base of the neck.

Norris tried to scream, and there wasn't enough air in his lungs to push it out. His fingernails tore at Chaplin's wrists, and they couldn't budge those relentless hands.

A hand gripped Chaplin's shoulder. "Do you want to kill him?" Edwards asked the question mildly enough.

Chaplin glared at him. "Stay out of my business."

"If you want to kill him go ahead. You're close to it. Look at his face."

The calmness of Edwards' tone drove sanity back into Chaplin's head. He looked at Norris, and the man's face was turning blue. His fingers no longer tore at Chaplin's wrists. His breathing was thin sounding like dry leaves rustling together.

Chaplin removed his thumbs. "I guess I don't," he said slowly. "Not right now."

The bluish cast left Norris' face as air rushed into his lungs. His mouth was open with the effort of breathing, and his tongue looked bloated and blackish. Edwards had spoken just in time. Norris didn't have much time left.

Chaplin staggered to his feet. The pain's teeth were growing nicely, and where before they nibbled they now took great bites. He felt the sting of air against his lacerated wrists, and a few of Sugg's kicks must have landed against his ribs to put that great, clamoring ache in them. His stomach rolled and churned, and he was certain he was going to be sick. But he couldn't be sick until he finished what he had to do here.

Sepulveda was sitting up, and his face was doughy. He shriveled as Chaplin's eyes rested on him. He held out his hands in supplication and begged, "Please, señor. No more. I am very sick."

"You'll be a hell of a lot sicker if you ever cross my path again," Chaplin grunted.

His cane lay on the floor, and he almost fell on his face as he bent to retrieve it. He straightened and turned burning eyes on Procela.

Procela tried to blend with the wall. "No, señor." His tone lacked a pitch of being a scream. "I did not want to fight you. They made me."

Edwards said softly, "He's not worth fooling with."

Chaplin gave him a hot glance. "Are you going to try to stop me on him?" He jerked his thumb toward Sugg.

Edwards looked at the wild hating in Sugg's eyes. "I guess it'll have to be done sometime."

Sugg said in that queer, squeaky voice, "He'll shoot me if I get a hold of you."

"My promise he won't," Chaplin said quietly. Edwards was right. It came to a head here or someplace else. He fought off the reaching sickness by gripping the stick tightly with both hands.

Sugg eyed the cane. How well he remembered it. A decision formed in his mind for his eyes filled with slyness.

For a big man he was quick. He grabbed up a chair and was rushing Chaplin in the space of a breath. He held the chair before his chest ready to raise or lower it. His intentions were plain. He would take the cane on the chair, then seize Chaplin. Once those powerful hands closed on Chaplin his cane would be useless.

Chaplin remained poised on the balls of his feet, and only his quickened breathing showed tension within him. He could thrust the tip of the cane into Sugg's belly, but he didn't want to merely maim him.

Triumph washed Sugg's face as he neared Chaplin. Another step and one blow of the chair would crush the white man's head. He raised the chair high as he rushed the last step.

Chaplin glided to one side and thrust out his boot. Sugg tripped over it, and his momentum carried him forward in broken steps. He fought to stay erect, but the tripping was too thorough. He fell on top of the chair, and its splintering seemed unreasonably loud in the silent room.

His scream of rage was a thin, animal sound as he wrenched a chair leg free of the wreckage. He whirled, and Chaplin struck. The stick made a sickening crunch against Sugg's shoulder, and his mouth opened in a soundless howl of pain. His left arm hung useless, and the red wildness was back in his eyes.

Chaplin retreated before Sugg's catlike stalk

cursing himself. This made the second time he had missed a vital blow. Sugg swung the chair leg in enraged frenzy, and Chaplin kept jumping back from it. He was already hurt, and avoiding those bull-like rushes was taking a terrible toll. He could feel the trembling in his legs, and his lungs were laboring.

He caught a glimpse of Edwards' anxious face and snapped, "Stay out of it."

The momentary inattention almost cost him dear. Sugg swung the chair leg, and Chaplin sucked in his stomach before its sweep. Even then the leg twitched at his coat.

The force of the blow pulled Sugg far forward, and his head was low enough for a shoulder-high swing. Chaplin wanted a better opportunity, but this might be the best he would get. He took a half step to the side and whipped the cane getting the leverage of his body behind it.

The cane caught Sugg squarely across the forehead, and it sounded like an overripe melon being dropped on the floor. Sugg's forehead shattered like a brittle eggshell, and still his vitality was enough to carry him forward for a couple of running steps. He hit the wall and bounced back from it. He spun, and his voice was a choked gargling. He was sightless, for the blood formed a red curtain before his eyes.

He fought falling. He fought it with an energy that was terrible to see. Then both knees unbuckled at once, and he plunged on his face.

Chaplin didn't put another glance on him. He had seen lifeless men fall before.

Procela looked at Sugg, then crossed himself. His shaking lips formed a soundless *Dios Mio*.

Chaplin was weaving as he walked to Edwards. "Get me out of here. I'm going to be sick."

Edwards' arm supported him to the street.

Chaplin's estimate was correct. He was violently sick, and not all of it went into the street. He looked at the stained front of his coat and swore in weak, helpless disgust.

Men rushed to him, and one of them asked, "What happened?"

Pride was evident in Edwards' voice. "He went in there and kicked the hell out of four of them. I heard the yelling and swearing and followed him. But he didn't need me at all."

Chaplin gave him a wan smile of gratitude. "Get the records, Haden. I'd say they were in that rawhide-covered chest."

He bit his lower lip. He was afraid he was going to be sick again in front of all these watching eyes.

Three men went back in with Edwards. They returned carrying the chest, and their eyes were awed.

"Jesus," one of them said. "He broke Sugg's head wide open. Norris can't sit up yet, and Sepulveda and Procela are afraid to."

Men surged forward cheering Chaplin. Edwards

caught the shine in Chaplin's eyes and understood it. His son-in-law had built for himself the respect of the town. It was an excellent start for a public official. He smiled at Chaplin, and his throat felt kind of tight.

Men insisted that Chaplin ride the chest back to the Administration House, and willing hands carried it. It was a jolting ride, but Chaplin doubted he could have walked the distance. It was a triumphal procession for everybody but him. He gripped the chest hard to keep his balance, and he fought the sickening waves that threatened to engulf him. Wouldn't it be a hell of a thing if he fainted and fell off of the chest?

He got down before the Administration House and faced the crowd. "The *alcalde*'s office will be open tomorrow. No more business today, boys."

He turned and walked inside, and he didn't weave too badly. He thanked Edwards silently for closing the door on the crowd. If that chair had been a step farther away he would never have made it.

He slumped into it and thought petulantly, Why is it getting so dark? Then the cold touch of a wet rag on his face pushed the reaching blackness back. He let Edwards sponge his face, and his head cleared with each touch of the wet rag.

Edwards dipped some water out of the olla and came back with it. Chaplin had been surveying himself. His clothing was a wreck. He doubted if his trousers could ever be cleaned, and his coat would have to be thrown away.

He drank the water and groaned.

Edwards asked anxiously, "Are you hurt pretty bad?"

"I'm not hurt at all," Chaplin snapped.

"You groaned like it," Edwards said suspiciously.

"I'm thinking of what Talitha will say when she sees me."

CHAPTER TEN

Chaplin found his new job to be arduous in three areas—his buttocks, thumb, and forefinger. His buttocks ached from long contact with a hard chair, and his thumb and forefinger cramped from writing endless words. He gloomily examined the inside of his second finger. He was right in thinking the skin was wearing thin.

People flocked into his office all day long wanting redress against this abuse, relief from that outrage. All of them had to be listened to, and all of them meant more paperwork. And Edwards was screaming for him to examine all the titles in the chest taken from Sepulveda's office. He snarled soundlessly. How many hours did Haden think he could crowd into a day?

He looked sourly at his finished work of the morning. The unfinished work beside it was much higher.

He sighed and drew out a fresh sheet of paper. He wrote rapidly, then scanned the finished form. It was an official document of the law. It was a little awing to realize he could haul in anybody he wanted and have them stand in fear and trembling before him, that his decision could so greatly alter their lives. This document read:

State of Coahuila & Tejas.
District of Nacogdoches.

Mr. John Cartwright.
You are hereby cited to appear at the Alcalde's Court to be held at Nacogdoches on the first Monday in March next, at the hour of 9 o'clock A.M. to answer to the complaint of Lewis Holloway, for five hundred dollars damages for taking forciful possession his lands. Herein fail not or judgment by default will be given against you.

C. Chaplin
Pr. Alcalde
Dist. Nacogdoches

He sighed and laid the document on the completed pile. Completed, he thought forlornly. It was just the starting. The court hearing was ahead. If the citations kept piling up at the rate they had piled up in the last ten days there wasn't going to be nearly enough days in his life to sit in judgment on them.

Behind him he heard Edwards roar at some new outrage and smiled wanly. Haden had found another discrepancy in the rawhide chest. For ten days he had been roaring like that at very short intervals.

Chaplin shook his head. He wished he had his old surveyor's job back, he wished he had its freedom. The law made life so damned complex. But without it the Gaineses, the Norrises, and the Sepulvedas plundered and robbed.

"Look at this," Edwards yelled.

Chaplin stood, welcoming the interruption. The few steps back to Edwards' desk eased the cramp in his legs.

"I've never seen such frauds," Edwards spluttered. "A blind man could see where they've altered the records. Gaines had it sewed up pretty tight with Sepulveda in office. He knew Sepulveda would rule in his favor regardless. My God, Chichester, we've got a lot of old crimes to straighten out."

Chaplin sighed as he envisioned the hours of confinement ahead of him that were necessary to straighten out the old frauds. And that didn't take into consideration how current affairs were piling up. Why damnit, he thought explosively, I'll never catch up.

Edwards waved the offensive record before him.

"I want a citation drawn up against Millton. I want him hauled into court."

Chaplin's temper was thin. He took a deep breath, and before he could say anything Judge Williams came into the office. There was urgency in his walk and face. "Have you heard?" he cried.

Chaplin felt the tightening of unease. It must be something important for Williams wasn't the type of man to become excited.

"Which particular thing am I supposed to have heard?" he asked.

"Saucedo's messenger just arrived in town. There's a rumor going around that Saucedo is throwing out the election and proclaiming Norris *alcalde.*"

"I don't believe it," Edwards thundered.

Chaplin cocked his head. That rumble outside like the distant sound of thunder was the concerted roaring of many men. It had a hungry, jubilant sound, and it seemed to be moving this way.

He walked to the window, and at the far end of the block the mob packed the street from building to building. He turned his head and glanced at Edwards and Williams.

"We'll know in a minute for sure," he said quietly. "You two stay inside."

He stepped out and waited for the mob. Norris and Sepulveda led it, and Chaplin guessed its strength at better than fifty men.

The memory of Chaplin's fight in Sepulveda's cabin was still clear for men shifted uneasily away leaving Chaplin to face Norris.

"You're out," Norris said triumphantly. "I've got a letter from Saucedo throwing out the whole election."

"And you're in, I suppose."

"I'm in," Norris said in a loud voice.

The men nearest him slapped at his back and cheered.

Chaplin gave him a long, speculative glance. "I want to see that letter."

Norris flushed. "Do you think I'm lying to you?"

"Don't tell me it isn't possible," Chaplin drawled.

The flush in Norris' face grew deeper at the burst of laughter from around him. He glared at the laughing faces, and the sound died.

He pulled a letter from his pocket. "Read it for yourself."

"I intend to," Chaplin replied.

He unfolded the letter and saw the seal of Mexico embossed upon the paper. He had no doubt the missive was official. His face was immobile as he read, and only the growing anger in his eyes showed his emotions.

The letter accused Haden Edwards of every election crime known. He had padded the ballot box, he had voted people who had no right to vote. He hadn't allowed the Mexicans to vote at all, and if he didn't discontinue abusing them Saucedo would take steps to see that he did. The letter wound up by ordering Edwards to turn over the office of *alcalde* with all its records to Samuel Norris.

Chaplin was tight-lipped as he handed the letter back. "It's your office. Come in with one man, and I'll turn over the records to you. I can't watch more than two of you, and I've got office supplies I don't want stolen."

Norris' eyes burned wickedly, but he made no comment as he and another man followed Chaplin into the building.

Edwards stared at them, and Chaplin said, "Saucedo's set aside the election results. I'm turning over the records to Norris."

Edwards sprang to his feet, and Chaplin stopped his outburst by warning, "Don't fight it, Haden."

He watched Norris and the other man pick up the rawhide-covered chest. He had spent a lot of skin to get that chest—and for nothing.

He waited until the door closed behind them, then looked at the pile of work on his desk. He swept it off with a savage sweep of his arm. That work had been wasted too.

Edwards said bitterly, "You quit. You let them walk in here and take the records without a fight."

Anger showed in Chaplin's face now. "I read Saucedo's letter. He believes you stole the election. You know who packed him full of lies.

But you wouldn't write him stating your side. Oh no. You didn't have to."

Edwards' face was dazed. "I didn't think it was necessary. I believe in honesty and justice. If a man lives by that he doesn't have to explain—"

"You're not in the States," Chaplin said violently. Edwards might have stopped this by writing Saucedo and presenting his side. At least it would have given Saucedo pause. He might even have sent someone to investigate what was really happening. At the moment Chaplin felt a vicious anger at his father-in-law. Edwards was too hardheaded to take advice.

He wanted to punish Edwards, and he said, "You wouldn't have turned over the records, would you? No, you would've fought them. Gaines would have loved that. That would have been an act of rebellion against Saucedo's order. He'd have sent the Mexican army to run you out."

Williams said calmly, "He's right, Haden. He did the only thing he could have under the circumstances. We'll have to wait until Saucedo learns the truth."

"I'll write him," Edwards mumbled. "I'll set him straight."

It wouldn't do any good now, Chaplin thought. He knew what the tone of Edwards' letter would be. Anger and outrage. Gaines had gotten in the first hard blow, and Saucedo would look at Edwards' letter as lies and excuses.

He started for the door, and Edwards asked, "Where are you going?"

Chaplin stopped and glared at him. "I'm going out to the camp. Didn't you know? I'm out of a job."

Talitha stirred in his arms and asked in a low voice, "Are you sorry?"

"In a mixed-up way. I'm not sorry to get out of that office. But I could've helped a lot of little people. God knows they're going to need it now."

"Maybe." The word carried no promise. It wouldn't change if Edwards didn't stop bulling his way through every rule and custom. It would never change if he didn't stop and make an honest evaluation of the situation then proceed accordingly.

"What are you going to do now?"

His arms tightened about her. "Can't you guess? I'll have more time to spend with you."

"Oh you," she said in feigned disgust. But her lips pressed softly against his cheek.

CHAPTER ELEVEN

Gaines watched a sullen-faced Sepulveda pack the last of his belongings for the move to the shed. He grinned and said, "Cheer up, José. It's not that bad. I told you we needed this place for an office."

Sepulveda wished he had enough daring to say,

"You could use the shed." If he had that much daring and Gaines answered him without exploding, Gaines would say, "The shed is too drafty."

Sepulveda thought bitterly, It is too drafty for an Americano but not for a Mexican. He felt lonely and sad. He was stripped of everything, his authority, his house, his easy life. If Saucedo wanted to protect his people it was time he moved now. He wondered what would happen if he wrote Saucedo and told him of his complaints. He let the thought slip away. Even if he could write it would be too dangerous.

"Don't leave yet, José," Gaines said. "I may have something for you to do."

He looked at Norris. "We've got the office, but it isn't doing us much good. The money's coming in too slow." He scowled at the scarred table top. He had offered to sell land to the settlers for ten cents an acre, two cents less than Edwards charged. The outlaws bought their titles from him, but the settlers avoided his office as though it had a large sign lettered "plague" on it. He had cornered one of them and asked about it. The man hadn't been afraid to speak up. He had said, "We're afraid of any title you can issue. I'll still get mine from Edwards."

He had to think of something that would bring in more revenue. He had to tax his brain, and— His eyes widened. That was it all wrapped up in a simple, little word. Taxes. By God, he had the authority. He could levy any taxes he wished.

"It costs money to run a government, doesn't it?" Gaines said.

Puzzled, Norris stared at him. If Gaines was talking about the kind of government they gave it hadn't cost them a cent.

"It sure does," Gaines said softly. "It costs money to keep up the streets, and we've been letting people use them without paying a penny. I say we got a right to levy a toll against every traveler who passes through Nacogdoches."

Norris' eyes went round. "You mean you're going to tax them for using our street?"

"Didn't I say it?" Gaines said indulgently. Once the idea had taken seed it rooted and fruited with amazing speed. "There's not a store in town that's bought a permit to do business. The saloons are selling Philadelphia whisky, El Paso brandy, New Orleans rum, and Tennessee white mule and not paying a cent in taxes, either on the bottle or by the drink. That's a lot of tax money we're losing."

Norris was getting the idea, for his eyes gleamed. "You figuring on taxing everything?"

"Everything." Gaines grinned. "We don't know how long it's going to last. That two-horse grist mill Lantrell brought in from St. Louis ought to be good for some revenue."

Norris picked up the chain of thought. "How about the sawmill?" It took one man sawing all day to get a single board out of those thirty-foot logs of loblolly pine. It would be slow, but that single board ought to be taxed.

Sepulveda's face was still mournful. They would make much money, but he didn't see where it would help him any.

Gaines laughed at his expression. "José, you don't think I'd leave you out, did you. You get over to Horatio Biglow's printing shop and tell him to print up some tax stamps. I don't care what they look like. Tell him to put George Washington's face on them or anybody else he's got." His eyes danced with delight. "And while he's printing those stamps tell him to print some extra ones that he can buy for running his shop."

Sepulveda's face remained doleful. He could see the future with bitter clarity. He would be nothing more than an errand boy.

"Get that sad look off your face, José. I've been thinking of making you a tax collector. You just be sure that too much of it doesn't stick to your fingers."

Joy beamed from Sepulveda's eyes. He would handle much money, and Señor Gaines would not be too displeased if a little of it stuck to his fingers.

"I go, Señor Gaines. I get the tax stamps very quick."

Gaines stood after Sepulveda left. "I've got to be getting back to the ranch."

A chilling finger traced a crawly course down

Norris' spine. "Wait a minute. You're not going to leave me here alone to face the town when this is announced?"

Gaines looked at him coldly. "What's the matter with you? You've got all the authority in the world. You're the *alcalde*, aren't you? You just be damned sure everybody pays. The first one who fails make an example of them."

Edwards' face was savage as he paced the office. Five strides one way, then back five. The floor drummed as he thrust his boot heels against it.

"Patience," he yelled. "You sit there and counsel patience while they're stripping the town to its bones."

Judge Williams smiled faintly. Haden Edwards' stock of patience was never very great. "You say you've written Saucedo about it?"

"Twice," Edwards yelled. "And not an answer to either one."

"He's hardly had time, Haden. Gaines and Norris are squeezing everybody. The Mexicans in town are hurting as much as anybody else. Their complaints will get to Saucedo. That will change his thinking." He hoped it would. Sometimes it took a long time to erase a bad impression, and Edwards had certainly made that with Saucedo.

Haden looked only at the dark side, but progress was being made. Supplies, escorted by armed men, arrived regularly, and new colonists still poured in. Edwards' machinery was working smoothly. Each new arrival got his land quickly, and while he was afraid to move onto it he worked with other men making preparations for the spring planting. It wasn't satisfactory though nobody grumbled too much. And given enough time this annoyance of Gaines' taxes would work out. It depended upon Edwards' patience.

"Can you see any other course, Haden?" Williams asked softly.

Chaplin came into the office in time to hear the question. He looked at Edwards, and it wasn't hard to guess at the topic of conversation. That was all Edwards talked about.

"Are you talking about taxes?" he asked.

Williams nodded. "I say it's only a temporary thing. Haden has to keep his head."

"I know what I should do," Edwards said. "I should throw Gaines and his crowd out of the country. I could take twenty men and clean them out for good."

"Do you approve, Chichester?" Williams asked.

"I'd like to be one of those twenty men. But the way Saucedo feels about us now we'd be nailing our own coffin shut."

Edwards turned his wrath on him for backing Williams. "Do you know Elisha Roberts is going back to Natchitoches? Our leading merchant is leaving because Gaines' taxes are taking all his profit."

"He'll come back," Williams said soothingly.

"If there's anything to come back to," Edwards muttered. He looked at Chaplin and asked pointedly, "What are you doing in town this time of day?"

Chaplin sighed inwardly. Edwards was a hard man to live with these days.

"I heard a report that the Dust brothers have been arrested."

"What for?"

"They bought two horses for five dollars apiece from Gaines. He charged them twenty dollars more for a tax stamp. They didn't like the deal. The report says Norris is going to make an example of them."

"They will like hell," Edwards snapped.

Chaplin smiled faintly. Ernie and Myrick Dust were big, hard-working men. Like a lot of big men they were slow to anger, but once that anger was aroused it could have some devastating effects.

"Stay out of it until we see how much help they need." Chaplin's eyes sparkled. What he hoped for was to see that famous Dust anger burst all over Norris. It depended upon what kind of punishment Norris had in mind.

Williams said from the front window, "A crowd's gathering before Stone House."

"So he's going to make a public spectacle of it," Chaplin murmured.

"Did you expect any other kind?" Williams

asked dryly. He smiled as Chaplin stepped aside for him and Edwards to use the door first. "Is that true manners, Haden, or is he bragging about how young he is?"

Edwards grunted. He was in no frame of mind for lighthearted jesting.

Chaplin pushed through the crowd gathered before Stone House. The Dust brothers were tied to a small post facing each other. They had been stripped to the waist, and Norris stood behind one, a whip in his hand, a gloating look on his face.

Chaplin could only see Ernie's face. It had a bewildered look as though the man couldn't fully comprehend what was happening. The crowd was mostly silent for there was hardly an individual here that hadn't felt the tax bite.

Edwards pushed up to where Chaplin stood, and Chaplin stopped him.

"Wait a minute. Let's see what happens." He didn't think either Ernie or Myrick would take a public lashing. Protest against abuse always started from an individual. Other individuals joined it until it swelled to a force mightier than a tide.

Norris drew back his arm, and the lash whistled through the air. It curled around a bare back, and Myrick groaned. Chaplin's lips tightened at the livid tracery of the reddening welt.

Norris moved around to lash Ernie. Myrick flung up his head as the pain spread through him.

Wildness was seizing his eyes, and his jawline was a bunched ridge of muscle. That big chest swelled, and the arm muscles bulged. The same idea entered Ernie's head for the same terrible wildness entered his eyes. They strained together, and the ties holding them to the post parted.

Norris watched them in petrified fear. He managed to get words past his dry lips. "Stop them," he yelled.

Nobody in the crowd was interested in stopping them. The Dust brothers were roaring in unison, and it had a hungry, animal sound.

They stripped the remainder of the cords from their wrists and leaped forward. Norris' decision to run came too late. He didn't take his third step before Myrick caught him by the shoulder. Ernie jerked the whip from his hand, and Myrick shoved him hard against the ground. An outraged arm swung, and the whip curled around Norris' neck. He screamed and tried to crawl from the punishment, and Ernie followed relentlessly. The whip beat dust out of Norris' clothes, and his screaming was a continuous thing.

He made his feet once and darted at the crowd. He had no sympathizers, and the crowd formed a solid wall before him resisting his efforts to force a passage.

Myrick tripped him up, and the whipping started all over. Norris lay on the ground, a whimpering, groveling thing. His face was crisscrossed with red welts. His clothes must have been beaten clean for the whip no longer raised dust from them.

Myrick yelled, "Give me that whip," and jerked it out of Ernie's hand. He laid it on with new enthusiasm, and Chaplin started forward.

Edwards threw out a restraining hand. "Let them cut him to pieces." His face was filled with savage enjoyment.

"If they kill him we'll get the blame," Chaplin answered and threw off Edwards' hand.

He stepped out and caught the whip arm before it descended. A head turned and fierce eyes glared at him.

Chaplin said gently, "I think you've made your point. If you kill him the Mexican government will be after you."

Sanity returned to those wild eyes. "Maybe you're right," Myrick muttered.

Ernie jerked at the whip. "Let me have one more lick at him," he begged.

Norris' whimpering sounded like a lost kitten's mewing. Blood seeped through his clothing. If he wasn't badly hurt, there was no doubt he was painfully so.

Chaplin said sharply, "You'd better get out of here, as fast as you can. When he collects his wits he's going to send somebody after you."

Myrick Dust muttered, "Makes sense to me."

Chaplin led them through the crowd, and no one tried to block their way. It had been a sudden turnabout, and most men looked at the two big men with a dazed respect in their eyes.

Their horses were tied a block down the street, and Chaplin asked, "You haven't paid for any land yet?"

Myrick shook his head. "We got a few personal things we might pick up. It won't take us long."

"Good. Why don't you try Austin's colony?" It was a shame to lose them. Haden Edwards needed men like these two.

They exchanged questioning looks, and Ernie nodded. "Sounds like we'd be right smart if we did. We just couldn't take no public licking," he added.

Chaplin smiled. "I sort of figured that way. Good luck." He watched them until they were out of sight.

Most of the crowd had already scattered. A couple of men were helping Norris to his feet. Norris was a good moaning man. Chaplin grinned as he heard him all the way here.

He walked back to Administration House, and Edwards and Williams had beaten him there.

"Did they get away?" Williams asked.

"All clear, Judge."

Williams smiled. "An excellent way of handling it, Chichester. The Dust brothers abused the *alcalde*. You had no hand in it. Nobody can pin a single shred of blame on you." He added slyly, "Though I don't think Haden fully approved."

"I didn't," Edwards said flatly. "I can't stand this

pussyfooting around." His face was darkening. "I say if a man's got a job to do let him do it and not depend upon somebody else."

Chaplin had a wry look in his eyes. That expression was familiar and how well he knew those opening words. Edwards was building up to another tirade.

Chaplin looked at Williams' amused expression and resigned himself. He was saved by Nathaniel Trammel's entrance.

Trammel was a lean, gangling native of Arkansas with a lazy walk and a voice equally as slow.

"I've been down to the Trinity River and looked over the ferry, Haden. Seems to be in fair shape. I'll take up the proposition you made me."

That erased some of the blackness in Edwards' face. Chaplin knew the ferry had been a source of worry to him. Under Edwards' contract he had to keep the San Antonio Road open across his grant and the ferries running over the deepest rivers. The last ferryman had died ten days ago of fever, and a dozen men had refused the job on the mosquito-ridden river. Trammel had said, "I'll look it over. People in Arkansas don't worry about a little thing like mosquitoes."

Edwards said, "Good, Nat. I think you'll find you'll make more than you figured on. Traffic will be getting heavier all the time."

"It's already heavier than I thought. I run it a

couple of days. 'Bout worked my arms out of the sockets hauling on that rope to get the ferry across. I hired me an assistant, a half-starved Mexican named Ignatius Seruche. He's tickled to death to get a chance to eat regularly. That all right with you?"

"It's your business. Run it any way you please."

Edwards waited until Trammel left. "I wonder what Gaines will make of this."

Chaplin knew he wasn't referring to the ferry. That was a small, unimportant thing. Edwards was talking about Norris' whipping.

CHAPTER TWELVE

Norris groaned every time he stirred in his chair. And he had to keep stirring for his bruised and lacerated flesh couldn't stand long contact with anything. He didn't think there was an inch of him the whip had missed.

Gaines grinned with malice. "Looks like you picked the wrong pair of boys to make an example of."

"I wish they were here," Norris muttered. "I'd kill them."

"But they're not." Gaines had thought hard about the incident trying to make capital of it with Saucedo. He couldn't see how it could be turned to advantage at all. It was too bad Edwards or Chaplin hadn't whipped Norris.

"Edwards put a new ferryman on the Trinity," he said.

Norris didn't care. All he could think about was his aches and pains.

"Trammel hired an assistant, a Mexican named Seruche." Gaines' eyes were alive with interest as he watched his brother-in-law.

"I don't give a damn," Norris said irritably.

Gaines snorted in disgust. "I don't know how you got along before you knew me. We've got another pin to stick in Saucedo's hide."

Norris stared at him with puzzled eyes.

Gaines shook his head. "I knew I'd have to spell it out for you. You write Saucedo and tell him Seruche owned the ferry. Trammel came along and saw a pretty good business. He took over the ferry and demoted poor Seruche to a helper. It's just another case of Edwards grabbing everything he can from the Mexicans."

Some kind of worry was in Norris' eyes, and Gaines asked, "What's eating on you now?"

"I'm thinking of all the lies we've written Saucedo. What happens if he comes up here and finds out they're lies?"

"You worry about the damnedest things. San Antonio is a long way from here. And Saucedo's too busy to even think about a poor town like this one."

"But he could send someone," Norris persisted.

Gaines' eyes grew cold. They always did at

opposition. "I vowed I'd run Edwards out. You watch me do it. You write that letter and get it off to Saucedo."

Chaplin was in the office when the courier from San Antonio came in and handed a letter to Edwards.

The man said, "I go back tonight, señor. If there's an answer—"

Edwards nodded. "I'll look you up."

When the door closed Edwards said, "Another one from Saucedo. I wonder what I've done now that displeases him."

Edwards was turning the letter over and over in his hands. Chaplin grinned. "You might open it and find out."

He watched the angry red color flow into Edwards' face as he read. This letter must really be a bad one to make Edwards look like this.

Edwards was swearing before he was halfway through the first page. Chaplin listened admiringly. He didn't know his father-in-law had such a command of oaths.

Edwards thrust the two pages at Chaplin. "Read it," he said in a choked voice.

Chaplin scanned the two pages. Saucedo referred to all of the old disagreements and added a new one. Edwards could not take a business from a Mexican citizen and give it to an American. He ordered Edwards to get Trammel off of the ferry across the Trinity and to return it to Ignatius Seruche. All of the revenues collected during Trammel's unlawful ownership were to be returned to Seruche.

Chaplin shook his head as he handed the letter back. "It's bad," he agreed.

"Bad," Edwards exploded. "Can't you see what it means? Any Mexican can take over anything owned by an American. If the Mexican was big enough he could even take over my entire grant." His face grew wilder. "Now tell me to show some more patience."

"Someway Gaines is behind this," Chaplin growled.

"Does it make any difference? If it wasn't Gaines it would be somebody else. Saucedo will believe anything told him. I don't want any more dealings with him."

"You've got to deal with him," Chaplin argued. "You've got to make him see things the way they are."

"And how would you go about that?" Edwards asked contemptuously.

"I'd drag Gaines and Norris down to San Antonio. I'd confront Saucedo with them."

The contempt in Edwards' eyes didn't lessen. "And they'd talk? They'd look at Saucedo and say everything you wanted them to say?"

Chaplin sighed. His solution wasn't worth a damn. He could beat the truth out of Gaines and

Norris here—but in San Antonio it would be a different matter. They would warble a different song the moment they were near Saucedo's force and authority—and Saucedo was already on their side.

"Then what are you going to do?" he asked.

"I don't know," Edwards said slowly. But something was forming in his mind.

Chaplin saw the reflection in the increasing glow in his eyes.

"Tell Talitha you'll be gone for several days," Edwards said abruptly. "We're going to take a trip."

Talitha wouldn't like that. Chaplin knew how stormy her eyes would look when he told her. He grinned and said, "You set me hard jobs. Where are we going?"

"To see Austin. I want to see how he's getting along."

Concern touched Chaplin's face. "And if he's having trouble too. What are you going to do?"

"I don't know," Edwards repeated.

Maybe he didn't know exactly, but he was skirting around something he was afraid to approach directly. Chaplin couldn't blame him. Rebellion was a frightening word.

San Felipe de Austin lay on the banks of the Brazos River. It was a neat, thriving town, and Chaplin contrasted it with Nacogdoches. It was a sorry contrast.

Edwards guessed at his thoughts and growled, "Austin was here a long time before I got my grant. And he hasn't had my troubles."

Chaplin suspected that Edwards was jealous of Austin's progress. On the ride down here Edwards had made a snide remark about a man who would name a town after himself.

Chaplin knew a little envy himself as he saw Austin's house. He thought of the tent he and Talitha lived in. How her eyes would glow if he could show her a house like this and say, "It's yours." That was a long way off for them, and he shook his head as he followed Edwards to the door.

Austin greeted them profusely. He had a knack of making a man feel welcome. No haggard shadow of worry was behind those large, piercing eyes, and Chaplin had a premonition Edwards wasn't going to find what he wanted down here.

"Sit down," Austin said. He ran a hand through his unruly, dark, curly hair.

It was an unconscious gesture repeated frequently. Austin was handsome, his features almost classic in their regularity. He had a quiet authority, and men would follow him. How marked was the contrast between him and Edwards. Yet both had the qualities of leadership. Only the matter of accomplishment differed. Austin was an *epée*, and its strokes would be delicate wearing its opposition down before it delivered the killing thrust. Edwards was a cavalry saber slashing with brutal directness trying to overpower the opposition from the first clash. It was probable that Austin would achieve his objectives more often than would Edwards.

Austin offered them whisky, and Chaplin sipped at his glass murmuring an appreciative, "Ah."

"You seem to be doing well here," Edwards said grudgingly.

Austin made a deprecatory gesture. "Everything seems smoothed out now. But we had trouble at first."

Edwards leaned forward, and his face was eager. "Yes," he invited.

"Our shipment of seed was delayed, and it made the first planting late. Then we had an outbreak of cholera. Dr. Heard saved a lot of our people."

Chaplin saw the disappointment in Edwards' eyes. This wasn't the kind of trouble he had hoped to hear. Cholera was a dread word. To cover an awkward gap Chaplin asked, "How did he treat it?"

"Ether, peppermint, and hot brandy toddies. He put the patient so close to a fire their feet were almost in it. He ordered a hot flatiron put on their chest and that somebody keep rubbing their hands." Austin smiled faintly. "Some of the survivors said they didn't know if that rough week was worth it or not."

Chaplin smiled in return. This was an entirely likable man.

Edwards asked doggedly, "You've had no trouble with Saucedo?"

Surprise showed in Austin's eyes. "None at all. In fact I've just received an additional grant for three hundred families."

The veins in Edwards' temples swelled. They always did when Edwards knew frustration.

"I've had trouble," Edwards said angrily. He poured out the long list of the abuses he had suffered sprinkling them plentifully with oaths against Saucedo.

A faint stiffening entered Austin's face as he listened.

Edwards finished by saying, "I'm convinced Saucedo is trying to get the Americans out. And if we don't stick together he'll do just that."

Austin's face went very still. The frightening word had not been said, but it hung ominously in the air.

Austin managed a wry laugh. "You don't mean that. You moved in on an old town in Nacogdoches. I know a lot of titles were already out, many of them forged I suspect. It was natural those squatters fight you."

"I can handle them," Edwards said hotly. "It's the Mexican government I can't handle." He asked a blunt question. "If I have to take extreme measures to protect my grant, will you help me?"

Chaplin saw Austin wince. Austin and Edwards stood on the opposite side of the fence, and each was convinced his view was the only one.

"Will you?" Edwards repeated.

He forced Austin into the only answer he could give. "No," Austin said. "I can only give you advice. If you'll only be patient—"

He used the wrong word. It washed temper over Edwards' face. "I've been patient too long," he said as he stood. "Now I'm going to do what I have to." He strode toward the door.

Chaplin shook his head and rose. Austin had a defensible side, and Chaplin couldn't blame him too much.

"I'm sorry, sir."

"I'm sorry too," Austin said. "Hold him down, can't you?"

Chaplin answered him with a bleak grin. Austin didn't know Haden Edwards very well.

He joined Edwards outside. It had been a long ride for such a short talk with no results.

Edwards said furiously, "He turned against his own kind."

"Maybe he didn't. He has a lot of Americans living in his colony. He has to think of them too."

"Are you defending him?" Those hot eyes probed Chaplin's face.

"No," Chaplin said wearily. "I'm just trying to look at things the way they are."

"I'm looking at them my way," Edwards said grimly. "I'm glad we made this ride."

Chaplin wondered why. Certainly not for the gains, for there were none.

Edwards answered the question in his eyes. "Because now I know I have to stand alone, and I can plan that way. I'm going to take steps to defend myself and my land. I'm leaving you in charge while I go back to Louisiana. I want my brother, Ben, to take over the army I'm going to raise."

Chaplin knew Ben Edwards well. He wasn't fond of the man. Ben Edwards had a successful military career behind him, and the memory of it made him pompous. In the War of 1812 he had swept superior British forces out of the Great Lakes area, and he could never forget it. It made him an authority on all military matters, and he flourished his opinion like a sword cutting through all opposition. Chaplin wished Haden wasn't so sold on the military mentality. That had been the trap that had ensnared him the first time with Jim Gaines. Let a man wave a military reputation before Haden's eyes, and he was awed.

"You don't approve?" Edwards challenged.

It really didn't make any difference whether or not Chaplin approved. Haden Edwards would go his bull-headed way.

He said shortly, "You're running it."

They rode a long way, an injured, angry silence

between them. Edwards' absence meant that all that administration work would fall on Chaplin, and he didn't relish the long confining hours in the office. He would also be responsible for the safety of the community, and right now the burden looked overwhelming. He didn't think now was any time for Haden to be going back to Louisiana, but saying it would only set Haden's mind the harder. For the first time he felt the presence of an ominous black cloud, and the chilling wind of failure blew from it. He had to say one more thing, and he searched carefully for the right words.

"Haden, don't rush into anything. Look every step over before you take it."

Edwards gave him an angry glance. "Don't I always?"

CHAPTER THIRTEEN

Chaplin stood in the doorway of the tent staring into the distance.

Talitha said, "Chichester," then in exasperation raised her voice as he didn't answer.

He turned his head and asked absently, "Did you call me?"

"Just three times. Do you know you're not fit to live with any more?"

He smiled and took her into his arms. "I can make you change your mind."

"You stop that," she said severely. She leaned

back against the circle of his arms. "You're worried, aren't you?"

"Yes," he admitted. "I wish Ben Edwards wasn't coming out here."

"You never did like Uncle Ben, did you?"

He considered that honestly. "Back in Louisiana I did. I could always move away when his stories of what he did in the war got too boring. That's going to be hard to do here. Haden's given him authority."

"That isn't the real reason, is it?"

"No," he answered. "This place is one big, opened powder keg." He made a sweep of his arm that included all of Texas. "Ben was never noted for his diplomacy. He's the lighted match walking in here. I keep shrinking from the coming explosion."

A tiny storm was gathering in her eyes. "Maybe there won't be an explosion. Maybe you're being unfair to him."

"You know Ben better than I do. You know how hardheaded he is. He's like—" He caught himself in time.

"Like Father?"

It was fearful how fast the storm in her eyes was growing. "They're brothers," he said doggedly.

She stepped back from him, and the storm was in full force.

"Ah come on, Talitha," he said, and a reflection of the storm was in his face. "I know you love your father. I do too. But he's not the easiest man in the world to live with."

She wasn't completely mollified. "I suppose *you* are," she sniffed.

He smiled at her telling point. "Maybe not," he conceded. "But I try to keep from rushing into things blindly."

"Like you did when you took the records from Sepulveda's cabin?"

He winced. Women had regrettably long memories. "That wasn't completely blind. I knew I'd probably run into a few of them in that cabin. I also knew what a lot of people in Nacogdoches thought of me. I was taking over an important office, and I wanted respect."

"And I threw away a brand-new coat. You get into trouble, and you say it's necessary. Father gets into trouble, and you say it's bull-headedness. I can't see the difference."

"It's there. After we talked to Austin I was convinced that Saucedo was trying to be fair as he saw it. I wanted Haden to ride to San Antonio with me and talk to Saucedo. It's possible Saucedo might have listened to us. He might even have returned with us or at least sent an impartial observer. It could have avoided a lot of trouble."

"Father refused?"

His expression was rueful. "With swear words. Haden's convinced Saucedo is against him. He's grabbed the first thing that came into his mind. Raise an army and fight him. And that's what Ben Edwards is coming out here for. Just let Saucedo get one little sniff of it, and we fight—or we're through."

The storm was gone from her face, and in its place was fright. She came back into his arms and he felt a shiver run through her.

"Maybe Uncle Ben won't come. He's getting old. Maybe he's too comfortable back in Louisiana."

"I wish I thought so," Chaplin said with a touch of grimness. "But he'll come. I've been looking for him the past week."

Somebody called, "Chichester."

He stepped to the tent entrance, and Jed Stevens was outside. At the far end of the compound a group of people were gathered around a new wagon. Chaplin sighed. He had thought he heard a wagon pull in. He couldn't see the driver, but he was sure who it was.

"Haden's brother is here," Stevens said. "He's asking for you."

"Tell him I'll be there in a minute." He moved back to Talitha. "He's here."

"Father's not with him?"

"I don't know. Stevens didn't say." To remove the anxiety in her eyes he said, "He probably stayed in Louisiana for some business matter. I'll be back and tell you as soon as I know."

"Ask Uncle Ben for supper."

Chaplin nodded. He was glad she couldn't see his sour expression. Her invitation meant a long and boring evening.

He crossed the compound, and his steps didn't have all the enthusiasm they could have had.

Ben Edwards stood in the wagon box, and if the journey had fatigued him it didn't show in his face. Chaplin thought he was a little fatter, and his hair had picked up more gray, but his cheeks were as ruddy as ever, and his eyes had that sparkling determination. He was looking the people over, and Chaplin felt an underlying displeasure in the man at something he saw. Ben Edwards had never had too much use for the civilian population.

Chaplin said, "Hello, Ben," and thrust up a hand.

Ben wrung it hard, then stepped down. "You're looking fit, boy. Talitha?"

"Fine," Chaplin assured him. "Talitha's expecting you for supper. You can use Haden's tent until he gets here. Is he coming soon?"

"He's lining up new settlers to bring in," Ben answered absently. He was looking about the camp, and Chaplin was sure there was a tightening about his mouth. The camp wasn't run on tight military lines at all.

"Talitha's been concerned about him."

"He's fine, fine," Ben's voice boomed. He whacked Chaplin on the back. "We're going to do great things here, aren't we, boy?"

Chaplin was afraid to ask what, though it loomed large in his mind.

"Talitha will be glad to see you," he said and pointed to his tent.

Ben turned and looked at Stevens. "Bring my wagon."

Stevens' face hardened at the pre-emptory order, and Chaplin said, "I'll take it, Jed."

Ben's lips pressed together before he blew out his breath. Chaplin half-expected him to raise hell about countermanding an order. Then Ben's face relaxed, and he stepped briskly toward Chaplin's tent.

Chaplin gave Stevens a faint grin and shook his head. He climbed to the wagon seat and turned the team. He took a deliberate time unharnessing the team and picketing them. Ben had grain in his wagon box, and Chaplin expected that. Ben Edwards was a thorough man.

He measured out portions of grain and saw the collection of weapons Ben had brought with him. Ben had enough weapons to stock an arsenal. Pistols, rifles, and swords were packed in the bed. Most of the weapons were antiquated, and Chaplin had no doubt that some of them had served Ben in the War of 1812.

He came back to his tent and found Ben and Talitha chattering animatedly.

"I never saw her look better, boy. Marriage agrees with her."

To cover her blush Talitha said, "Uncle Ben says Father is bringing in several hundred new families, Chichester. Isn't that wonderful news?"

Chaplin groaned inwardly. He was snowed under by paperwork now. Haden Edwards was an incurable optimist. He never admitted, even to himself, that their position could be in danger.

"You've got a rabble here, boy," Ben said patronizingly. "But I'll whip them into shape."

Chaplin gritted his teeth. He'd break out into a howl if Ben used that "boy" again. "They're farmers, Ben. Not soldiers. You can't expect too much."

"I've made soldiers out of their kind before."

Chaplin said in a grumpy tone, "You brought enough weapons to arm all of them." He wanted to whittle on the man. "Most of them look too old to use."

Ben laughed. "Place your dependence in the tried and trusted, boy. You won't be let down that way."

Chaplin sighed. Ben Edwards hadn't changed in the slightest degree.

"What are your plans, Ben?"

"Haden and I mapped them all out. I'm going to raise and train our own army. Then let Mr. Saucedo try to cram something down our throats."

"You're talking about rebelling?"

"If necessary. A smart man is always prepared."

That was another one of those damned platitudes. "Ben, let me ride down and see Saucedo," Chaplin said earnestly. "I think most of the grievances can be cleared away by a little honest talk. Austin isn't having any trouble."

Ben frowned at him. "You mean compromise with Saucedo? Don't you know compromising is a sign of weakness?"

Chaplin thought savagely, why didn't you stay in Louisiana and sit on your fat ass? This pompous, old fool was going to wreck everything beyond repair.

"Haden approves of everything you're saying?"

"He does," Ben boomed. "We talked it over at length, and he's letting me do the planning."

Chaplin cursed Haden's worship of the military. Ben Edwards may have covered himself with laurels in a past war, but they were old and musty now.

Talitha had a worried look on her face. "Uncle Ben, if you would listen to Chichester. He's been here. He knows—"

Ben chuckled. "I like to see a wife defend her husband. But Chichester sees things through a young man's eyes. He doesn't have the age that gives him mature judgment."

Oh my God, Chaplin thought wildly.

"Haden knows you're overworked, Chichester. We're going to keep you in the office," Ben said. "While I'm training the army we've got to keep peace around here. I'm turning over the Regulators to Colonel Parmer."

"Who's Colonel Parmer?" Chaplin asked dully.

Ben looked astounded. "You've never heard of Colonel Martin Parmer, the ring-tailed panther? I was lucky to get him to come out here. He's a legend far beyond his native state of Missouri. He's hunted bears with a knife, and once he killed a panther by swinging it around his head by the tail. If you want to know about him ask the Indians. They know and fear his name. He'll be here in a few days."

Another wild man, Chaplin thought. With legend and fact about him so intermingled it was impossible to separate them.

"He'll put some order in this country," Ben said.

"But the Regulators have been part of Chichester's job," Talitha objected.

Ben smiled at her. "And I'm sure he's done the best he could. But it takes a military man to understand and handle these matters."

Chaplin had to get some air, or he would choke. He mumbled inarticulate words and plunged for the entrance.

Ben looked at Talitha and raised his eyebrows. "What's bothering him?"

She said defensively, "He hasn't been feeling well."

"He looked sickly to me." Ben bobbed his head.

"I told you before you married him he was a frail man. It's a good thing I arrived when I did."

Talitha's eyes flashed, but she managed to hold her tongue. She hoped Chichester wouldn't go to the tavern. In the mood he was in he might get roaring drunk. She shuddered as she thought of what he would say then to her Uncle Ben.

CHAPTER FOURTEEN

Norris looked apprehensive as he said, "Jim, that Parmer caught the last wagonload of slaves. He freed them and killed four of the boys."

His face was gloomy as he listened to Gaines swear. He knew Gaines would make it sound as though it was all his fault.

Gaines turned the air blue. Norris was wise enough not to attempt to interrupt him. Gaines finally caught a breath and yelled, "Can't any of you do anything right?"

"We had scouts out," Norris said defensively. "Parmer ambushed us."

"You bring those scouts to me," Gaines said ominously.

"I can't. They're dead."

Gaines' face was ugly mean. "And the rest of you ran?"

Norris held out his hands helplessly. "What else could we do? We were outnumbered four to one."

"And you were out in front of the runners,"

Gaines sneered. He paced the room, his face working with his heated thoughts. This was the third shipment of slaves Parmer had intercepted. He was going to have to be much more careful in his planning of the next shipment.

"Next time—" he started.

Norris shook his head. "There won't be a next time, Jim."

"What do you mean?" Gaines yelped.

"I mean I couldn't get enough boys to make another raid into Louisiana. They're scared of Parmer, and I don't blame them."

He thought Gaines had exhausted his supply of oaths. He was wrong.

Gaines ran down and caught his breath. "I ought to go into town and blow his head off."

Malice shone in Norris' eyes. "Why don't you do just that?" Sure they needed somebody to plan these things, but Gaines always stayed under cover taking none of the work or risks.

"We had a profitable thing going," Gaines said bitterly. "And you botched it."

Norris looked sullen. It wasn't true, but it would not do any good to deny the botching.

Gaines pulled on his fingers, popping the joints. Sometimes he felt as though everything was closing in on him. Look what had happened to his tax scheme. After Norris had tried to whip the Dust brothers, more and more resistance had appeared. And Sepulveda was a hell of a poor collector. He had begged instead of demanded, and each refusal had strengthened the town's backbone. It took money to keep even as loose as an organization like his going. If he didn't keep the men in tobacco and whisky money, at least, they'd drift on him—or worse, go over to Edwards. For a while he had been dipping into his own pocket, and those had been sad days.

The old days were gone. There was no doubt of that. None of the outlaws dared raid a wagon train like they used to. The tax scheme had failed, and now Parmer was breaking up this new business.

Gaines scowled. Handling slaves was the most profitable of all his schemes. Of course he couldn't call them slaves for Mexico had abolished slavery. But he had found a way to get around that. It had started small, and he had hit on it quite by accident. An escaped slave had come to him for help, and just a few days before Gaines had talked to a farmer who had said he would give a hundred dollars for a good field hand. Gaines had apprenticed the slave to the farmer for ninety-nine years. The hundred-dollar cost was to come out of the slave's wages along with his board and room. It had tickled Gaines. With the small salary the apprentice earned he wouldn't pay off his indebtedness in nine hundred and ninety-nine years. When the escaped slaves had come in too slow he had organized raids into Louisiana bringing in slaves by the wagonload and charging whatever he thought the planters could bear. He had collected as much as five hundred dollars for some of the huskier slaves. Now Parmer had smashed all that.

Norris said hopelessly, "Jim, it looks like everything's turning against us."

"You didn't stop running soon enough," Gaines said contemptuously. "You should've kept on until you ran clear out of the country."

But everything was going to keep turning against him as long as Edwards remained in the country. If he could get Edwards thrown out things would return to normal. His eyes narrowed. He'd better concentrate on that until it was done.

He made another turn of the room, then stabbed a finger at Norris. "I want a Spanish grant made out. You've got enough old paper. Make it look real impressive. Make it out to Edmund Quirk." He walked to a small chest and pulled out a faded and torn map. The *alcalde*'s office wasn't of much value any more except that it still retained all the records. He studied the map and said, "Make out that grant for the Aes Bayou district." His finger traced the outline of the grant he wanted.

Norris studied the map. He said in a small voice, "That's over a hundred square miles of the best land in Edwards' grant."

Gaines grinned wolfishly. "Isn't it," he agreed.

"Edwards already has families settled on that land."

"Drive them off."

"Parmer will put them back with his Regulators."

"That's right. And Saucedo will blow sky high. Edwards won't even recognize good Spanish grants now, and his contract says he has to. I think this will drive Edwards out of Texas. Take some of the boys and get those families off. You're not afraid to do that, are you?"

Chaplin stood in the tent entrance and watched Ben drilling a large body of men. Ben barked unending orders at them, and their shuffling feet kept a pall of dust over the encampment. The men's faces were sullen, and Chaplin wondered how long it would be before they openly rebelled.

Talitha said in an exasperated tone, "I wish he'd stop that. There's dust over everything."

"I wish Haden would get back," Chaplin said gloomily. Ben had taken charge of everything, and he had an inexhaustible vigor. He wore out men much younger than himself.

Talitha moved to him, and he put an arm about her shoulders.

"You're worried, aren't you?" she asked.

"Yes," he admitted. "We came here to develop land and put families oil it. That's been about stopped. All Ben thinks about is training his army." Bitterness crept into his voice. "And Haden is raising more families to bring out here."

"He's doing what he thinks best."

Chaplin caught the stiffness in her voice and dropped the subject. It was only natural she defend her father. She couldn't be expected to see where Haden had gotten off the main road.

He kissed her and said, "I'm going down town." He didn't want to. It would be another long day filled with more of that cursed paperwork.

Parmer was waiting for him at the office. The man wore well. Chaplin liked him better all the time. Parmer could consume more whisky without effect than any man Chaplin had ever known. He was a big, robust man with an insatiable appetite for excitement. His sparkling blue eyes always contained a restless seeking for it.

He said, "I'd go crazy tied to this."

"I am."

"How'd you like to come with me? A bunch of Twilight Zoners ran thirty families off their land in the Aes Bayou district. We're going down there to put those families back."

A new light filled Chaplin's eyes. "Let's go," he said.

Parmer took a hundred men with him. As they rode out of Nacogdoches, Chaplin had the feeling their every movement was being observed.

Parmer rode beside him and asked, "How do they think they can get away with this?"

"That's what's got me worried," Chaplin answered.

Parmer gave him a piercing glance, then shrugged. He never questioned the reason for any activity; he just welcomed it with open arms.

They camped that night, and Parmer secured his camp. Chaplin admired his thoroughness. Nobody was going to surprise Parmer. Even a wily Indian couldn't get close to the picket line.

Chaplin lay on his back and stared up at the sky. The night was soft and warm, and the stars hung just overhead. The months had slipped by without him fully realizing it. Sure a lot had been accomplished, but so much more remained to be done. It was good, bountiful country, and it would bless a man if there was ever peace long enough for him to work it. He had once seen hot springs bubbling in a mud flat. The bubbles exploded with little pops. What they were doing was chasing the little pops when they should have been searching for the springs. He smiled bleakly as he thought of telling that to Ben, and fell into a troubled sleep.

It took two more camps to reach the Aes Bayou district in the southernmost corner of Haden's grant. Parmer held up his men as he surveyed the first cabin. The sun was strengthening on the maturing crops around the cabin, and it sparkled on the dew on the leaves.

Parmer said, "It looks harmless enough. Let's go." He stood in the stirrups and waved his arm forward.

Chaplin wouldn't have moved in so recklessly.

He felt nakedly vulnerable as they approached the cabin. Parmer didn't know how many riflemen could be concealed behind those walls.

Somebody shouted, "There he goes," and Chaplin saw the horseman burst from behind the shelter of the cabin.

"Run him down," Parmer ordered, and a dozen riders took after the lone man whooping as they rode.

"They'll catch him," Parmer said. Disappointment was in his voice. "It isn't going to be much of a job if it's all this easy."

The cabin was empty, and it had been thoroughly looted. Even the furniture had been carried away. Several bottles had been smashed against the floor. It looked as though quite a celebration had been going on here.

A voice called, "Colonel, they're bringing him back."

Chaplin stepped outside with Parmer and saw the horsemen bringing the man back. His hands were tied behind his back, and his eyes were bloodshot. His clothing was filthy, and his last washing must have been just a dim memory.

"Know him?" Parmer asked.

Chaplin shook his head. "He's one of them."

Parmer grinned. "That's not hard to tell. We'd better keep on the windward side of him."

"Cut him loose," he ordered.

The man sat in the saddle rubbing his chafed

wrists. His defiance was a poor mask, for his eyes darted fearful glances at the ring of hard-faced men.

"Get down," Parmer ordered.

"You got no right busting in on a man's house thisaway," the man blustered.

"You never owned a house in your life." Parmer reached up and grabbed an arm. A jerk spilled the man out of the saddle, and he crashed heavily against the ground. "I gave you an order." Parmer's tone might have been discussing the weather.

The man looked at him with frightened eyes. "They had no right to go off and leave me. Just because I was sleeping it off." His voice dropped to a whisper. "What are you going to do with me?"

"Probably hang you," Parmer said cheerfully. "Unless you want to tell me what you were doing in that house."

"It's mine," the man insisted.

"Get a rope," Parmer ordered.

Chaplin didn't get a chance to find out whether or not Parmer would have gone through with it.

"It was given to me," the man shouted. "Honest it was."

"I doubt that. Who gave it to you?"

"Edmund Quirk."

Parmer shot a questioning glance at Chaplin, and Chaplin shook his head. He didn't know the name, but that didn't mean anything. There were dozens of names out there in the Twilight Zone he didn't know.

"Where did Quirk get it?" Parmer asked.

"He had an old Spanish grant giving him a hundred and four square miles."

Parmer whistled as he looked again at Chaplin.

"Probably a forgery," Chaplin said. "If he had a legal title to it it would have turned up before now."

Parmer prodded the man on the ground with his boot toe. "Why were you here?" he repeated.

"Honest, Quirk gave it to me. All I had to do was to live here for a while."

"Your living here is ended. Bring him along," he ordered.

The man's eyes were insane with fear. "I told you everything I know. You can't hang me."

"We'll take you back to Nacogdoches and throw you in jail. Maybe you'll remember a little more."

He waited until the man was tied to his saddle before he mounted. As he rode off he said to Chaplin, "I've got a hunch we won't find anybody else."

Parmer's hunch was correct. The remainder of the houses sat in brooding silence, their interiors thoroughly sacked.

"I think it's safe for the families to move back on," Parmer said to Chaplin. "I think it was just a looting mission."

He saw disagreement in Chaplin's face and challenged, "Don't you?"

"There's more behind it than that," Chaplin said slowly. "I've got a feeling we've walked right into a trap."

Parmer shrugged. "Remind me to worry about it."

Parmer was just leaving the office as Chaplin entered. He grinned and jerked his head toward the rear of the room where Ben Edwards was sitting. "The old man is hot because we didn't bring in more prisoners."

"You can't bring in what you can't find," Chaplin said shortly. Ben had kept him outside cooling his heels while he talked with Parmer. Chaplin resented the handling.

As he sat down beside Ben's desk Ben said, "I've given orders to Parmer to move those families back onto their land. And to keep an eye on them."

"Maybe that's what they wanted you to do," Chaplin said curtly.

Ben raised his eyebrows, and Chaplin snapped, "I don't think those men ever wanted to occupy that land. And I think we did just what they figured."

"Gaines and Norris?"

"Who else?"

"They won't be active much longer. I sent a long

letter to Saucedo telling him we're through standing for such things. I listed all the abuses he's allowed and finished by telling him I've ordered Gaines and Norris to be shot on sight."

Chaplin's lips formed two soundless words— my God. When Ben tore something he tore it from top to bottom.

"Do you know how Saucedo will react?"

Ben shrugged. "I don't give a good damn. I'm tired of pussyfooting around with him. It's time to take a stand against tyranny." His eyes had the shine of a zealot.

Oh Lord, Chaplin mourned. "Have you sent the letter?"

"It's gone." Ben nodded with satisfaction. "I'm going to make Haden's grant a small republic. I've already thought of a name for it. Fredonia. If we establish liberty here it'll spread to the other American colonies. I've had reports there's not a thousand Mexican troops in all of Texas. They won't fight against American arms. When Austin joins us—"

"He won't," Chaplin said flatly.

"He will. I've just started a letter to him. Let me read what I've got so far." Ben cleared his throat.

"If it be permitted to the bounded intellect of man to fathom the beneficent desires of an Almighty Providence we shall be compelled to believe that a political millennium is

159

approaching, when the thrones of despotism shall be prostrated, the fetters of mankind unbound, and slaves, by a resurrection as miraculous as that which shall raise our molded dust into eternal life, exalted into freemen."

He raised his eyes waiting for Chaplin's approval.

Haden, Chaplin mourned, why did you send this bombastic fool out here? He asked, "When Austin gets that do you know what he'll think? He'll think you're a madman."

Ben's eyes turned cold and remote. "Are you telling me not to send it?"

"I'm not telling you anything," Chaplin snapped. Nobody could do that.

Ben Edwards drew himself up to his fullest height. "You're with me, or you're against me."

"Have it any damn way you want," Chaplin snarled and stalked out of the office.

CHAPTER FIFTEEN

Haden Edwards returned three days later, and he was in high spirits. "I signed up a hundred more families, Chichester. They'll be here in a couple of weeks."

"You'd better be thinking of some way to send them back." At the startled flash in Haden's eyes

Chaplin asked, "Haven't you talked to Ben yet?"

"I've talked to him. He said you had a little disagreement."

Chaplin snorted. "He's openly talking rebellion. He sent a letter to Saucedo to that effect, and he wrote Austin in the same vein."

Haden's sigh was long and mournful. "I was afraid it would come to that. It just broke earlier than I expected."

Chaplin stared at him. The man wasn't even attempting to probe all the avenues open to understanding.

"Austin won't join you," he warned. "He won't jeopardize what he has because Ben went crazy."

"Ben's my brother," Haden said stiffly.

Loyalty was a fine thing if it wasn't misplaced. But Haden's trust was ridiculous. He had let Ben fashion this misshapen monster, and he would do nothing to put it out of existence.

Chaplin lost his temper. "Tell me it's smart to warn somebody of what you're going to do before you're ready to do it."

Haden's face was flushed. "Ben acted as he saw it. He has more experience than either of us."

Chaplin said a vulgar expression. Haden's eyes were beginning to snap. This argument would wind up by them shouting at each other if one of them didn't soften.

Chaplin thought, It's going to have to be me. "At

161

least let me ride down and talk to Saucedo," he pleaded.

"I have done nothing I shouldn't have," Haden said stubbornly. "Have I?"

"No," Chaplin admitted. But he also hadn't done many of the things he should have.

"I've got a right to defend myself," Haden went on. "All I have to do is to take a stand, and Saucedo will back up."

"And if he doesn't?"

"Then we'll whip him."

His values were always in bold colors. The subtle shadings never existed for him.

"And the other *èmpresarios* will join me. Austin, De Witt, the rest of them. All we have to show is a united front. Look how small and scattered the Mexican army is. Mexico City won't spend too much time or money trying to hold Texas. And we'll get help from Louisiana. You know how they feel about being up against a foreign state."

He sounded like Ben's parrot, and Chaplin knew it would be a waste of words trying to argue with him.

He stood and said, "If Austin and De Witt don't back you, God help you."

Even that didn't shake Haden. "It's not even coming to that. You wait until we get Saucedo's next letter. He'll be singing a different tune."

Chaplin refrained from shaking his head.

Sometimes Haden Edwards didn't know the real world existed.

He talked to Talitha about it a long time that night.

"What do you think will happen?" she asked in a frightened voice.

"War," he said. "Ben and Haden won't believe it. They can't see if Mexico backs down here she backs down all over Texas."

He felt the shiver run through her as she clung to him.

Ben and Haden Edwards had embarked on a wild and reckless gamble. They might have a chance to win it if all the imponderable ifs fell into line. Parmer had capable men in his Regulators, and the number would be swelled by the green men Ben had been drilling. But it was still a puny force against the might of Mexico. They needed Austin and De Witt, they needed Americans from Louisiana.

"What are you going to do, Chichester?" she asked.

"Why I'm going to stay," he said simply. "And do what I can."

The letter from Saucedo came ten days later. Chaplin was in the office when Haden received it. He saw the blood leave Haden's face, and the shock tightened his lips.

He resisted the savage impulse to swear at him.

163

The letter was evidently a terrible blow, but how could the man have expected anything else?

"It's from Blanco," Haden said hoarsely. "Saucedo turned the matter over to higher authority." He handed the letter to Chaplin.

Chaplin read it rapidly. It started off with a list of the old charges, all of them based on lies, then stated that the government had lost all confidence in his fidelity, that he had no right to be dictating laws as a sovereign. It wound up with a direct order that Haden and Ben Edwards get out of Texas. They were to surrender all claims to Haden's grant and leave Texas at once. There would be no trial, and if they wanted to protest this action they could appeal to Mexico City from the United States.

Chaplin handed the letter back. "You're not leaving." He made it a statement.

Haden shook his head. He was still in shock, and his lips barely formed the words. "I can't leave. I've got more than fifty thousand dollars of my own money tied up in this. A fortune's at stake. By the time all eight hundred families get here I'll receive more than four hundred thousand dollars in administrative fees. Then there's the land that was promised me for my own. Better than a hundred and eighty thousand acres. Land around Natchitoches is selling for five dollars an acre. It'll be worth as much here. I can't leave."

Haden Edwards stood to gain more than a

million dollars. It was a vast, incredible sum. It pointed him down the only road he could go.

"What are you going to do, Chichester?"

Chaplin put a mournful thought on what might have been. He too had been put on a road which he had to follow. "Why I'm staying," he said steadily. "And doing whatever you need."

Haden reached out and wrung his hand. Color had returned to his face and with it a new assurance. "I'll get Ben and Parmer in here, and we'll talk this over. Ben will get a letter off to Austin right away and—"

Haden was a stubborn man, unwilling or unable to learn from his past experiences. Ben had already written too many letters.

Chaplin interrupted. "Let me ride down and see him."

Haden considered it. "That might be best," he conceded.

Haden, Ben, and Parmer were in the office when Chaplin returned from seeing Austin. It had been a long and hard ride, and both rider and horse showed the effects of it. The talk with Austin hadn't lasted ten minutes. Chaplin had been unable to budge him in the slightest. At the end Chaplin had lost his temper and snapped, "We're fighting your battle too."

"Not mine," Austin had disclaimed stiffly. "I had no part in the making of it."

Three eager faces swung toward Chaplin as he entered. The eagerness slowly faded. They didn't need Chaplin's shaking head to know the trip had been a failure.

"He wouldn't listen," Chaplin said flatly. "He wrote Saucedo saying he had no part in this. And he's warned De Witt to stay out of it."

"I didn't expect that," Haden said, and for a moment he looked stricken.

Ben and Parmer grinned at each other. Ben briskly rubbed his hands together. "We don't need him."

Chaplin stabbed a finger at him. "Suppose Austin throws in with Saucedo? He might to protect what he has."

Ben looked incredulous at the suggestion, then an angry flush mottled his face. "Ridiculous," he snapped. "An American fighting against an American?" His jaw jutted out like a granite outcropping. "If he does we'll run him out of Texas with the rest of them." He banged the desk with his fist. "By God I'll write and tell him so."

Chaplin sighed. It was a sorry thing that Ben Edwards had ever learned to write.

Parmer said, "Let's see how many men we can figure on. Say two hundred from my Regulators. Two hundred more farmers." He threw a questioning look at Haden. "They'll fight to save their land, won't they?"

"They'll fight," Haden replied.

Parmer's slow, lazy grin showed. "I wouldn't call that a big army. We've got to do better than that."

Haden said, "Ben, write Elisha Roberts in Natchitoches and ask him to raise some volunteers. He's got no reason to love the Mexican government. Their *alcalde* drove him out of Nacogdoches."

Parmer's eyes glowed. "We ought to be able to count on a couple hundred more men from there. We're still a little shy."

Haden swore softly. "I never thought of them until now. Dr. Hunter and his Indians. He tried to get land for them, and the Mexicans wouldn't listen to him. If I give him land he'll give me an army."

"Indians, huh?" For a moment Parmer looked dubious, then he said, "Why not? How many can this Hunter produce?"

"Five hundred anyway," Haden said recklessly.

"That would give us more than the Mexican army in Texas. We're going to whip the hell out of them. We'll draw them out into the open and stretch their supply lines. With the Indians cutting those supply lines to pieces the Mexes will be helpless. They'll give up in a week's time."

"Suppose they won't leave their garrisons?" Haden asked.

"Then we starve them out. We'll pick us off a garrison at a time. By the time a couple of them give up the rest will be running for Mexico."

Chaplin looked at the beaming faces. They reminded him of three children playing war games. They had it all figured out on paper, and the war was won. But there was one, vast difference between children and them. When children tired of their game they could walk away from it with no following consequences. These three had stepped into a giant trap, and it would take a lot of prying to open its jaws.

"What's our first official act?" Parmer asked.

"I'll get off a proclamation of freedom to Saucedo," Ben said.

Chaplin said dryly, "I think the first thing we ought to do is to take over authority in our own town."

Parmer eyed him keenly, then nodded with approval. "He may walk slow, but he walks sure," he said. "Let's go arrest us some men."

"You'd better take some of your Regulators," Haden advised.

"I think Chichester and me can handle it," Parmer drawled. "We don't want to tip them off."

He threw an arm about Chaplin's shoulders as they walked out onto the street. Chaplin thought with grim amusement, at least one of them thought he was capable of handling a share in this.

The *alcalde*'s office was empty. Papers were strewn about the cabin floor, and everything pointed to a hasty flight.

"They're gone," Parmer said in disappointment.

Chaplin nodded. He hadn't expected to find

Gaines here, but he had hoped to bring in Norris and Sepulveda.

"Well that's the last of them," Parmer said.

Parmer was wrong. Chaplin was sure they would see those two again.

When they returned Haden asked eagerly, "Are they in jail?"

"They ran," Chaplin said. "They guessed at what we were about, or they got word someway."

"Did you bring back the records?"

"You've got something more important to think about now than those records."

For a moment argument was strong in Haden's face, then it faded. "Maybe you're right," he muttered.

Chaplin thought it would be a long time before those records were important again. And during that same interval he was cut free of all paperwork. War was a drastic way to end it but highly effective.

"Chichester, go find Dr. Hunter," Haden said. "Take the Yokum brothers with you. They're damned good Indian men. Ask Hunter to come down here for a conference."

"I'll leave in the morning."

Chaplin looked back at the door. The three had their heads close together again. The first, official act of rebellion had just been committed, and it hadn't sobered a one of them. He shook his head and closed the door softly behind him.

CHAPTER SIXTEEN

Talitha was loathe to let him go in the morning. She said, "Riding into that awful Indian country—" and shivered.

He was a little worried about that himself, but he didn't let it show on his face. "Honey, when they find out why I came they'll welcome me with open arms."

He kissed her, and she snuggled closer in his arms. "Chichester, I wish sometimes we'd never came to this terrible country."

"We'd miss all this excitement," he said dryly.

She had a thought in mind, and she wouldn't let go of it. "It was safe back home. A person could go on with their plans. We could have even started our family by now."

"I've got a little time," he said. "We could start one now. I'm not that rushed."

She pushed him firmly out of the tent.

How he loved that beautiful color in her face. He smiled and said, "We'll take up that subject when I get back."

She looked for something to throw at him, and he ducked in mock terror. No other woman in the world had eyes that could sparkle like hers.

The Yokum brothers were waiting for him at the edge of camp. One could see no family resemblance between them. Eric Yokum stood over six feet tall with light coloring and pale blue eyes. Quincy Yokum was a good six inches shorter with hair and eyes as black as a crow's wing. But both were alike in nature, quiet, almost reticent men listening instead of talking. Haden was right when he called them good Indian men. They passed freely through Indian country without seeming to give it much thought.

Chaplin said, "I'd like to ride down and see Ellis Bean before we find Hunter."

The Yokums gave it thought before Eric answered him. "Might be a good idea. He's the Mexican government's Indian Agent for Texas."

Now that was news. Chaplin's respect for Bean increased. "Does he know his business?"

"He knows it," Quincy grunted.

Bean might be an agent for a foreign government, but he was still an American. Chaplin didn't know where his loyalty lay, but he was going to try to feel him out.

Bean's soldiers eyed the three men indifferently as they rode into Fort Teran. A few of them smiled, and their eyes were warm and friendly. It was a disturbing thought to Chaplin that in a short time he could be shooting at them and they might be returning it with equal ferocity.

Bean said, "Howdy, boys. Put your butts down."

The Yokum brothers' eyes flashed as Bean poured three glasses of whisky. They seemed at home here. Bean grinned as he set out a much larger glass for himself. "It's my whisky," he explained. "And I'm selfish."

The four men sat for a few moments in companionable silence sipping at their drinks. Chaplin had been here before. Bean served excellent whisky.

"Did you hear what happened in town?" he asked.

"I heard you took over Nacogdoches. Norris was by here early this morning. He looked like he was running scared." His eyes probed Chaplin's face. "You know how that's going to set in San Antonio?"

"I know," Chaplin murmured. Bean knew or guessed what was in Haden's mind. Chaplin saw no reason of withholding anything.

"That's not all we hope to take over," he said gravely.

"Do you know what you're doing?" Bean asked gruffly.

"I hope so." Chaplin asked the question in his mind, asked it bluntly. "Where do you stand?"

Chaplin's directness brought a grin to Bean's leathery face. "I'll tell you something. I've got too many scars already. All I want to do is to live out the rest of my life on my land in peace. I stand with the winning side."

Chaplin smiled. That was frank enough. "And you have doubts about our side."

"I don't think you've got enough manpower," Bean said flatly.

"If Hunter brings in his Indians?" Chaplin asked softly.

"Ah." Those piercing eyes stabbed at three faces in return. "What are you going to promise him in return?"

"Land. All the land he wants for his tribes."

"It's a big bait," Bean said after a moment's reflection. "Can Hunter unite them, Eric?"

Eric Yokum weighed the question before he answered. "He'll do a job if he can bring Fields and Bowles together."

Bean nodded. "Cherokee chiefs," Bean explained to Chaplin. "Bowles is pretty jealous of Fields. I don't know whether or not he can swallow that jealousy long enough to help the common good. And there'll be trouble with the Kickapoos. They just don't like Americans. They remember the abuses they suffered in the War of Eighteen Twelve. If Hunter can wipe all that out he might be able to lead them."

He put an ominous doubt on the success of Chaplin's trip, but at least he had given Chaplin information. Chaplin wasn't going in as blind as he had been.

Chaplin said, "Thanks, Ellis."

"Sure," Bean said gruffly and walked to the door with them. He shook each hand in turn. "Good luck."

As Chaplin rode away he realized Bean hadn't committed himself in any way. All he had to cling to was that simple "good luck."

They visited a half-dozen Indian villages before they found Hunter. Chaplin was glad the Yokums were with him. While he couldn't say there had been open hostility the burning intentness in those watching, black eyes bothered him. If the Yokums noticed it they didn't comment, and Chaplin was ashamed to bring it up.

Once Quincy said, "They're on hard times." At Chaplin's questioning glance he explained. "Didn't you notice how few dogs we've seen? If an Indian village is prospering it'll be filled with dogs. When food gets scarce the dogs go into the cooking pot. The braves aren't hunting, or game's scarce. Did you see a single new tepee?"

"I hadn't noticed," Chaplin confessed.

That might have been disgust in Eric's grunt.

"All old tepees," Quincy went on after grinning at his brother. "Poorly patched with hides too cracked to be waterproof. Didn't you notice how hollow-eyed the squaws were? And none of the kids were playing. Signs of hunger."

Eric said thoughtfully, "They're going to be easy to deal with—or damned hard."

Quincy grunted agreement. "We'll have to feel our way."

They found Hunter in the Cherokee village of

Richard Fields. Dr. John Dunn Hunter was a tall, saturnine man with a hawk nose and brooding, black eyes. Some people' said he was a hundred percent Indian, others that he was a breed. Chaplin thought that the Indian blood predominated. It showed in the high cheekbones and in his coloring. His clothing was poor and hard worn, and Chaplin doubted if the man was aware or cared about it.

Hunter gave them no sign of welcome. He stared at them a long time before he asked, "You wanted to see me?"

"I'm Haden Edwards' son-in-law," Chaplin said.

A little of the hostility faded from Hunter's eyes. "I spent a great deal of time with him in Mexico City. He helped me all he could." The memory seemed to be softening Hunter. "I vowed once I would never trust another white man. Haden Edwards changed my mind."

Chaplin sighed inwardly. A moment ago he wouldn't have given much for his chances of even getting Hunter to listen to him.

He squatted on his heels and drew aimless marks in the dust with a stick as he talked. He told about the rebellion and of Edwards' promise to the Indians if they joined. He looked up at Hunter and finished, "You can name the land you want. Everything north of Haden's grant."

He had made it a simple proposition, and he let it rest there. He met Hunter's probing stare unwaveringly.

Hunter said abruptly, "Tell Edwards I'll bring some of the chiefs down to Nacogdoches to see him."

Chaplin let out a carefully held breath. Hunter had been walking on a knife edge of decision. He could have toppled either way.

Stephen Austin looked at the assembled throng in his village. He saw all those apprehensive faces, and apprehension was deep in his own soul. What he was about to say came hard, but for the good of these people before him it had to be said—and acted upon.

He held up his hands quieting the crowd. "You know I sent James Cummings to Nacogdoches to try and talk sense into Edwards' head. Maybe I'd better let him tell you what happened." He extended a hand and assisted Cummings onto the raised platform.

Cummings took a deep breath. "They're madmen at Nacogdoches. They want war."

Austin heard the voice of the crowd. A small voice now with the edge of anger nibbling away at the greater body of unease. It could be swelled into a great voice with all the unease consumed. It depended upon him. He had gone over his decision a hundred times, and he could see no other answer. But still the torment remained. Those were Americans at Nacogdoches.

"Edwards is trying to get the Indians to join

him," Cummings went on. "He's ready to arm those savages and turn them loose on every settler."

The crowd voice had more volume and more anger. The fear of the Indians was an ever-present one. This one point alone condemned Edwards to every man who was listening.

Austin put only half his attention on what Cummings was saying. He had heard from Saucedo yesterday. Saucedo and Colonel Ahumado would leave San Antonio soon with two hundred men to march to San Felipe de Austin. It was a pitifully small force. If Edwards struck them before they reached here he could wipe them out. Not only Edwards but any American force. For a moment the thought of independence lodged in Austin's mind. He dug it out and threw it away. Saucedo had been more than fair with him. A man did not turn against his friends because another lost all sanity. He was quite sure Saucedo would expect him to supply men for the march against Nacogdoches. Now he had to put his decision into words and convince these waiting men.

Cummings was through, and Austin nodded to him. He said, "Until Haden Edwards is driven out of Texas none of us will know any peace. Saucedo is ready to march with an army. I say we join him and end this threat to our security for once and all."

The silence didn't last long. Just long enough

for men to digest the words. Then the roaring swelled, enthusiastic and vociferous.

Somebody in the crowd yelled, "Hey, Stephen, are we taking Marley Waller?"

Austin smiled faintly. Marley Waller was a brass four-pounder cannon. Even the walls of Stone House in Nacogdoches couldn't stand against its bombardment.

"We're taking Marley," he said.

Men whooped and danced in the street. Austin watched them, and a sickness grew in him. He couldn't drown it with assurances that he had made the right decision—the only decision, he corrected gloomily.

CHAPTER SEVENTEEN

Haden Edwards received Chaplin's news with enthusiasm. "If Hunter agreed to ride here he'll join us. You can bet on that." He paced about the office, and there was vigor in his stride. "Ben got the letter off to Roberts. I know how Elisha feels. He'll raise us an army. We're going to win this, Chichester. Then we can go on with our business."

Chaplin thought, He looks younger. Fighting was the fountain of youth for most men. A sip of it put vitality in them and strengthened tired bones. Haden could very well be right, and Chaplin almost grinned. The bold excitement of this was reaching out and gripping him.

"When do you expect Hunter?" Haden asked.

"Right away. He wants to move on this as much as you do."

Chaplin felt the restlessness invade him. Parmer was out on some mission, and Ben was at his eternal drilling.

"What do you want me to do?"

Haden's thoughts were on something else, and he said impatiently, "I don't know. You might report to Ben."

Chaplin would be damned if he would. Ben wasn't going to stick a rifle in his hands and march him about.

He walked outside, and the afternoon's fading light was gray and depressing. The wind was chilly, and he shivered as he felt its teeth. Well, a man could expect the weather to be like this at the end of November.

A voice hailed him from across the street, then Jed Stevens came on a run. Something more than just that short dash put the panting in him.

"Chichester, me and Hamilton were out hunting. We saw Gaines, Norris, and Sepulveda camped in a ravine."

The restlessness was all gone. "You're sure?"

Stevens' nod was indignant. "I got eyes."

"How many men with them?"

Stevens said vaguely, "About twenty, I'd say."

"Did they see you?"

"Not us. We eeled away from there in a hurry."

Chaplin reflected a moment. Twenty men should be enough to capture Gaines and the others. The odds would be about even, but the advantage of surprise would tip the scales in Chaplin's favor.

"Jed, how'd you like to go out there and bring them in?" he said.

Stevens' eyes went round. "That's Colonel Parmer's job."

"He's out on scout. If we pull it off you'd be a big man around here."

Stevens said eagerly, "I'm with you."

"Raise twenty men without anybody knowing about it. Meet me on the west edge of town."

It was almost dark when they rode off. The sky was overcast, and there wasn't a glimmer of starlight to guide them. Chaplin hoped Stevens knew the country well.

He kept asking, "How much farther," and Stevens kept muttering, "Not far." But the way he kept peering ahead worried Chaplin.

"Ah," Stevens said in relief as a pinpoint of light showed on the horizon ahead. "That's it."

Chaplin gathered the men around him. "We'll walk our horses from here on. I don't want a sound until we get on the ravine's bank." He thought of something and asked, "Is it steep, Jed?"

"Just a swag. We can ride over it with no trouble."

"Good. We'll hit them on horseback. Don't shoot unless you have to. I want them alive." He

180

thought of Haden's face as he saw the captives and grinned. He'd show Haden he didn't have to place all his reliance on Ben and Parmer.

It seemed an eternity before he reached the campsite, and he kept expecting a yell of discovery. But Gaines ran a sloppy camp for he had no sentries out.

Chaplin waved men to the right and left of him, and surely those in the ravine could hear the muted thump of hoofs against earth and the tiny creaking of saddle leather. He saw men silhouetted against the fire, and while he couldn't make out their faces he was sure he saw Gaines' figure.

He looked up and down the line. The dark shadows were all in place. He roared, "Now," and spurred his horse down the sloping bank.

He heard the concentrated yelling as the line surged forward and saw men by the fire look up in shocked disbelief. To them it must have looked like a solid wall of horseflesh rushing at them.

The freebooters' horses squealed and reared in panic snapping the picket line. Some of them galloped into the running men, and that added to the panic.

Chaplin bowled a man over with his horse and wheeled it sharply back. He was looking for Gaines, and only pure chance would guide him to him.

Men were on the ground, and some of them

must have belonged to him for he saw men exchanging blows. The scene on the floor of the ravine was utter confusion. Human and animal screams blended, dotted by the heavier grunts and swearing. So far not a shot had been fired, or at least in the excitement he hadn't been aware of it.

He slipped his boot from the stirrup and kicked at a face as he drove past it. The boot toe met resistance, and he heard a hoarse yell suddenly blotted out. But the face disappeared. He was looking for Gaines, and how was he going to pick him out of this melee?

He clubbed a man to the ground with his rifle barrel, and that dash carried him well beyond the fire. He spun his mount and saw a man running for the far bank. The man turned his head, and the firelight was strong enough to recognize Gaines.

Chaplin yelled and spurred his horse forward. When he got close enough he intended to spring from his saddle and pull Gaines down from that bank.

His attention on Gaines was complete, and he didn't see the riderless horse galloping at him from an angle. The horse was running in blind panic, and it didn't swerve. It smashed into Chaplin's animal and staggered it. He kicked both feet out of the stirrups and was ready to leap if his horse went down. Somehow it survived the impact. It ran for a dozen broken strides, then it was in balance again. By the time Chaplin got it turned back on course there was no figure against the opposite bank of the ravine.

He rode up the bank and cast back and forth against the ravine's edge. He needed motion for only motion would let him pin Gaines against this black night.

Gaines was a wily man. He knew movement would give him away, that running wouldn't carry him any place against a horse. Chaplin's swearing grew more intense as he scoured the ravine's edge in short sweeps. He knew futility and frustration as he thought that Gaines could be hidden within a few feet of him.

He jerked on the reins as he heard a shot followed by three others. It was turning into a gunfight in the ravine, and he'd better join it. As he came back to the ravine he saw one of the outlaws with an aimed rifle at some indistinct figure farther up and snapped off a shot.

The rifleman dropped as though his feet had been kicked out from under him. He was dead before he hit the ground, for an outflung arm was close enough to the flames to feel their searing heat. The arm didn't move.

Chaplin heard a few more shots and looked for a target. Everybody he saw were his own men, and he prayed that a shooter knew his target before he pulled the trigger.

Stevens came toward him, a broad grin on his

face. "We made us quite a haul, Chichester. Come over and see what we got."

There were still forms dotting the floor, and Chaplin asked, "Anybody hurt?"

"Just them. Hamilton got a shoulder wound."

It was almost a clean victory at very little cost. If only Gaines hadn't gotten away. By now the man had taken the time to better his concealment, and Chaplin thought it would be useless to search for him.

Stevens was right when he said they had made quite a haul. Seven men were lined up against the ravine wall, and their faces were anxious as they looked at the ring of rifles covering them.

Chaplin's eyes glowed as he saw Norris and Sepulveda. "Well, well," he drawled. "Two of the big ones didn't get away. Tie them up. A lot of people in Nacogdoches will be happy to see them."

Norris had a sullen look, and Sepulveda's dark eyes were filled with pleading. "Please, señor," he begged. "I do nothing."

A sudden thought struck Chaplin. It still might be possible to head off the clash with Saucedo. If Sepulveda would write Saucedo and tell him of Gaines' machinations perhaps all problems could be ironed out.

"But you're going to do something," Chaplin promised. "You're going to write to Saucedo and tell him about all the lies he's believed."

"José," Norris said warningly.

Sepulveda's face was filled with apprehension. "Señor, I do not write."

"Then I'll drag you down to San Antonio, and you can tell him face to face. There's ways of making you do it."

Sepulveda shivered. The Americano's smile had a terrible quality to it. He knew what Chaplin meant—he meant torture. In the end Sepulveda knew he would agree to anything Chaplin wanted. Wasn't it logical that he do it now and save himself all that punishment?

Chaplin saw the defeat in his face and grinned. "I thought you'd see it the right way."

They caught up all the loose horses they could find. Some of the captured men had to ride double. One of the horses was burdened with the collected weapons. Most of the rifles were old, slow, and untrustworthy. Chaplin would make a present of them to Ben.

It was nearly midnight when they rode into Nacogdoches. Only the saloons were lighted. Word spread about Chaplin's capture, and more and more men rushed onto the street.

The laughing, exuberant faces were in the majority, but Norris and Sepulveda still had sympathizers for there were many somber expressions in the crowd.

Haden and Ben ran up to the scene, and Haden asked eagerly, "Is it true? Did you capture Gaines?"

Chaplin shook his head. "I thought I had him. But he got away in the darkness."

Ben said sternly, "I didn't authorize you to go after these men."

Chaplin said a vulgar expression, and Ben's face reddened.

"I didn't have time to find you," Chaplin said. "Did you want me to let them slip away?"

"No," Ben said lamely. "But as commander-in-chief of the Fredonian army I should know where my forces are."

Chaplin was weary of the pompous, little man. "This part of your forces is going to take the prisoners to jail."

Ben had to salvage something from this, and he said, "I'll take care of them."

Chaplin put a piercing stare on him. "See that they're well guarded."

Ben bristled. "I took charge of prisoners before you were walking well."

Chaplin said solemnly, "I've got that in mind."

But he let Ben take over and march the prisoners off to jail. He walked away with Haden and told him of his thinking concerning Sepulveda. "I think we might get Saucedo to reconsider," he finished.

Haden's expression was doubtful, and Chaplin said fiercely, "Isn't it better than war? Or because Ben wants war so bad do you have to, too?"

For a moment Haden's face flushed with anger.

Then he muttered, "I guess it's better your way."

Chaplin threw his arm across his shoulder. "We might just pull it off." He didn't know how much time he had left and maybe it wasn't enough. But he had to try.

He turned his head at the burst of gunfire from the street followed by gales of laughter. Nacogdoches was celebrating its first victory, a small one to be true but still important.

Chaplin said, "I think I'll join them for a while." He knew how they felt. It seemed an eternity since he had had something to celebrate.

He took a step and asked, "Coming, Haden?"

"Later maybe," Haden answered.

It was the beginning of a wild and noisy night. Men whooped and danced in the street, and if anybody had any serious intentions of sleeping they must have cursed the gunfire.

Chaplin had five drinks. He kept count of them because Talitha was alone. If he took the sixth one he wouldn't be concerned about it—until in the morning when he would be contrite and sorry.

He shook his head firmly at the offer of more drinks. He pushed aside the restraining hands and walked steadily out of the place. He turned his footsteps in the direction of camp, feeling quite proud of his virtue. He had checked the guard Ben had placed about the log jail. It was more than adequate though the men grumbled at not having a part of the celebration.

He quickened his stride. Talitha would want to know all about the event, and there would be renewed hope in her eyes when he told her of how he intended using Sepulveda. They would talk for a while, then the talking would subside. The blood was singing in his veins again. Very few men were fortunate enough to have a woman whose wonder never dimmed.

It wasn't possible but the celebration was still going on in the morning. Men were bleary-eyed and staggering, but if they were still on their feet they could still drink. Chaplin stepped around a half-dozen, sprawled, snoring forms in the street. Life in Texas was hard, and he couldn't blame them for trying to prolong their illusionary escape from it. But oh they'd pay a price for it. He grinned at the thought of the sick, depressed men when this celebration was over.

A man staggered into the street ahead of him, raised his pistol and shot a hole in the sky. From around the corner a volley answered him. Some of the spirits in town were still going strong. Chaplin suspected they had wasted enough ammunition to fight a small war.

He stopped at the jail first, and the sight of the man lying before it quickened his pulses with anxiety. Another form sat propped up against the jail wall, his lips bubbling soft snoring. Chaplin swore at the sleeping guards. They hadn't left their posts, but they hadn't missed the celebration. He walked around to the rear of the jail, and two more guards were out. And the back logs of the structure had been pulled loose leaving a gaping hole. His swearing burned his mouth. He had an insane desire to stomp the sleeping guards and controlled himself with effort.

Instead he turned and rushed to Administration House. It wasn't hard to figure out how the escape had happened. Norris and Sepulveda had sympathizers in town—hadn't he seen their faces last night? They had simply plied Ben's guards with liquor until they were insensible, then pulled out the back of the jail. Chaplin wasn't quite sure what he would do when he saw Ben, but he had to see him.

Haden and Ben were in the office. Both of them were red-eyed and dull. They had taken part in the celebration.

Chaplin cursed Ben until he was breathless. "You took over last night," he yelled. "And your guards let Norris and Sepulveda escape."

He expected wrath in Ben's face, but the man was too beaten of spirit.

Ben looked at the floor. "We'll go after them," he mumbled.

"Where?" Chaplin demanded. They didn't even have a starting direction, and Norris and Sepulveda had the advantage of hours of start.

"There goes our last chance to stop a war," he

said bitterly. "I could've made Sepulveda tell Saucedo the truth."

Ben shot him a brief glance. "Nothing's changed. We go right ahead as we planned."

It was too bad Chaplin couldn't choke this bumbler here and now. Before he could say the hot words crowding on his tongue Stevens ran into the office. Stevens looked like a rough night, but his eyes were filled with excitement.

"A bunch of Indians are riding toward town," he announced. "The boys are worried about it."

That would be Hunter and his braves coming in to talk to Haden Edwards.

"You go out and tell them not to worry," Chaplin ordered. "They're coming in to join us against Saucedo."

Stevens whooped and raced out of the office.

"Are you two clear-headed enough to talk to Hunter?" Chaplin demanded.

That pulled a glare from them, and a grin twitched at his lip corners. It faded when he heard the rattle of gunfire. Volley after volley crashed, and he said, "Oh my God."

He ran out onto the street, and a man was just raising his rifle to the sky. Chaplin knocked its barrel aside before the trigger was pulled.

The man looked at him in amazement. "Hell," he protested. "I was just welcoming them."

Chaplin whipped about and saw the Indians just a little beyond the edge of town. They sat milling, plunging horses, and they were on the edge of flight.

Another volley rang out, and the majority of the Indian party turned and fled. They were bolting a town that asked them here, then fired on them. Maybe a dozen of them still held their ground, but they were undecided. It wouldn't take many more shots to send them after their fleeing brothers.

Chaplin ran to the nearest horse, jerked its reins free and vaulted into the saddle. Before he kicked it into a hard run he yelled at a group of men, "Stop that goddamned firing." He raced toward the remaining Indians.

He swung his arm frantically as he rode, and the small party held.

Hunter was furious when Chaplin reached him. Three of the Indians held menacing guns on Chaplin. Their eyes kept darting to the town. No one else was riding out here after them.

"You asked for this conference," Hunter snapped. "And then you shoot at us."

"Wait," Chaplin pleaded. "The gunfire was a welcome, not a threat against you. Everybody in town is glad you're here."

Hunter's eyes were knives stripping the cover from Chaplin's heart. "We'll go in and listen," he growled finally. "I warn you if it's a trick the entire Indian nation will wipe out your town."

"No trick," Chaplin assured him. He looked toward the fleeing Indians. They were mere dots on the horizon. "There's no way to get them back?"

"None," Hunter said in flat denial. "Some of them will never join you now. Their pride has been wounded."

He swept his arm forward, and the Indians fell in behind him.

Chaplin saw mixed emotions on the faces in town. He saw glowering distrust and fear, he saw elation and relief. A few months ago all those staring faces would have tried to wipe out the Indians on sight. Now their leaders told them they were allies. It would take more than the mere saying of words to make men fully believe it.

He leaned against a wall in the office and listened to Hunter and Haden Edwards talk. The Indians, for the most part, sat with impassive faces, and he didn't know whether or not they understood the talk. He was particularly interested in Richard Fields, the Cherokee chief. The man had an intelligent face, and Chaplin had the feeling Fields tested and weighed every word Haden spoke. Chaplin wished Bowles was here. Bowles might be only a minor chieftain, but he led the opposition to Fields. Hunter had warned him that Bowles would probably do the opposite of what Richard Fields did. Chaplin thought wryly, It is impossible to get men, even of the same race, to agree on a single thought.

Haden Edwards said, "I promise you all the land

north of my own grant on a line beginning on the east at the Sabine River and running straight west to the Rio Grande."

"How far north?" Fields demanded.

"To the land bought by the United States from France."

Fields nodded. Chaplin couldn't tell whether or not it was approval or merely a gesture signifying he understood.

It was a stirring offer, and the scowl left Hunter's face. Hunter and Fields exchanged a glance, and Chaplin would have given anything to know what was in their heads.

Hunter stood and said, "I will take your offer back to the tribes."

Haden looked disappointed, and Hunter gave him a frosty smile. "Did you expect agreement from one talk? All I can do is to tell the tribes about it."

Fields spoke up unexpectedly, "The Comanche and Tonkawa will be difficult."

Hunter nodded, but it put no distress in his eyes. He had his dream too, dreams of ample land for his people, and he looked beyond minor obstacles to fulfillment.

"How soon will I know?" Haden couldn't keep the urgency out of his voice.

Hunter shrugged. At times he seemed all white man, then his Indian blood took over. Now he was Indian, and he couldn't be pushed.

"Thirty days. Maybe sooner."

Haden gnawed his lower lip. He wanted to plead. It showed in his eyes. He was wise enough not to push against Hunter's stolid expression.

He and Chaplin watched the Indian delegation ride out of Nacogdoches.

"Quit fretting," Chaplin advised. "He can't go any other way but to join you. He knows the Mexicans will never give him any land."

"I wished I knew," Haden muttered.

Chaplin didn't blame him for his worry. There seemed to be a gathering tide, and it was running against them. They had lost Austin's support, and Norris and Sepulveda had escaped. Now part of the Indians had been alienated by the town's welcome. Was Hunter's influence strong enough to overcome it? Chaplin hoped so.

He felt the gathering storm all around them. A man didn't need the actual devastation of the wind to know that a storm was here.

CHAPTER EIGHTEEN

Ellis Bean poured another glass of whisky for his guest. Joseph Harter amused him. He was an educated man with pretensions of being a doctor. But Bean had had far-reaching sources of information. Harter was nothing but a fraud. His malpractice had caught up with him in Mexico City, and he had been run out of the country. He had stopped at Fort Teran in need of food and water, and Bean had let him stay several days. He would probably let him stay until Harter ran out of fresh stories.

"Edwards just might pull it off," Bean said. "He had his meeting with Hunter. Hunter has to go along with him. With the Indians Edwards might be able to run the Mexicans clear out of Texas."

Harter couldn't care less, but Bean cared. He had to be on the winning side, or his land could be in jeopardy.

He said, "I think I'll ride in to Nacogdoches and have a talk with Edwards. Want to come along?"

Harter shook his head. It was comfortable here in Fort Teran, and Nacogdoches had nothing to offer.

Bean grinned. Harter had a fresh bottle of whisky before him. That should keep him occupied until Bean returned.

He stepped outside the house and found Sixto Mendoza, the sergeant in charge of his twelve-man detachment of troops.

"Sixto, get your men together. We're taking a little trip to Nacogdoches."

Mendoza's eyes brightened. Life at Fort Teran could be a boring thing. "An official trip, señor?"

Bean grinned. "You might call it that."

"Then we will wear our best uniforms." Ah, it

was a delight to see the way the señorita's eyes flashed at the sight of uniforms.

"You do that. And tell the men they just might have some time off there."

Bean laughed as he saw Mendoza dash away. Soon there would be many barked orders. He thought he'd better take his hired hands along too. Twelve men wouldn't make too imposing a retinue, and he wanted Edwards to be impressed. He wanted Edwards to open up and talk to him, for if he was going to make the best deal he could he had to know all the details.

War hysteria swept Nacogdoches. The timid settlers were leaving with their families for the security of the States. The threat of war had its depressing effect on prices too. Houses that had recently sold for eight hundred dollars were being offered for fifty and found few buyers.

Haden raged every time he saw a wagon leaving. He watched a small train of six wagons pass before Administration House and cried, "Look at them. Running before even a shot is fired." He couldn't understand how men could value their land so little.

"Let them go," Chaplin repeated for the half-dozenth time. "This will shake out the weak and get them out from underfoot." It was hard to keep masking his concern over the defections. It seemed so many were leaving. Haden had relied upon at least two hundred of the farmers fighting with the Regulators. He wondered how many of that number were left.

Nacogdoches was filled with the two-way traffic. Chaplin only hoped that it balanced out, that the men streaming into town eager for a fight replaced the departing ones.

He turned from the window. "Where's Ben?" he asked idly. He didn't care. It was a relief to be away from the man.

"Out trying to talk some fight into some of the weak-kneed ones," Haden replied.

Chaplin doubted that Ben would get many recruits. Ben's patience was too thin, and at the first sign of unwillingness Ben would flay the man with his tongue. If he wanted to influence men Chaplin would send somebody other than Ben Edwards.

He heard a yell from outside and turned back to the window. Some excitement had hit the town for men were running. Chaplin saw Parmer dashing toward the town square.

"Something's up," he said and flung open the door. He ran out into the street and stopped a passing man.

The man shook his head at Chaplin's question. "All I know is that the colonel wants us in a hurry."

Chaplin ran with the man to the square. Parmer stood in the middle of it shouting orders. Men raced to and fro gathering weapons while others tightened cinch straps.

Chaplin caught Parmer's arm. "What is it?"

Parmer stopped long enough for a brief answer. "Scouts report the Mexican army on its way here. Just a few miles out of town now."

Chaplin's amazement showed. The Mexican army couldn't have reached here from San Antonio. It didn't have enough time. He cried, "It couldn't be."

"They're out there," Parmer said impatiently. "You coming along? I've sent a messenger recalling Ben and his men. We'll have enough to stop them."

"I'm coming," Chaplin said and ran for his horse.

Thirty men galloped out of Nacogdoches to meet the oncoming enemy. To their left a cloud of dust was boiling up on the horizon. Chaplin suspected that Ben Edwards and the men with him were making that dust racing on a tangent with Parmer toward the same goal.

Parmer raised in the saddle and pointed. Chaplin nodded. He had already seen the small force less than a mile ahead of them. He would guess no more than twenty-five men in it. It couldn't be more than a scouting detachment at the most. The sun reflected against the crossed white straps on the uniform breasts. Those were Mexican soldiers all right. And no matter how small the number, crushing or capturing them would be a blow to Saucedo.

He yelled and spurred his horse to greater speed.

The detachment ahead had halted watching the onrushing charge. Chaplin wondered if the unexpected shock of it had frozen them into immobility or were they holding their ground preparing to fight? If so he didn't think much of their location. It was too easily surrounded. To his left rifle fire crackled, and it was picked up all along the charging line. He left his own rifle in the boot. It was useless firing at this distance.

The band ahead wheeled and bolted. Cries of elation swelled from the charging men. The Mexicans were fleeing without a shot coming close to them.

Parmer swept his arm forward, gesturing follow them. Chaplin thought it useless. With that lead they'd never overtake them. But he fell in with the pursuit. A suspicion grew in his mind after a couple of miles. That last turn confirmed it. They were chasing Ellis Bean and his detachment at Fort Teran. He tried to shout the information at Parmer, but Parmer couldn't hear him or was too engrossed with his pursuit to leave it.

Bean and his men were well-mounted. They increased their lead and rode into Fort Teran with better than a mile advantage. Parmer had trouble restraining his men. They wanted to make an assault on the fort then and there.

"What were you yelling at me?" Parmer asked.

"That was Ellis Bean we were chasing," Chaplin said grimly.

Parmer's expression didn't change. The name meant nothing to him.

"Bean could help us or hurt us. He's got a lot of influence with the Indians."

Parmer grinned. It had been a comic chase, and he couldn't take it seriously at all.

"All right. Go in and tell him I'm sorry. If he'll come back to Nacogdoches I'll buy him a drink."

In his earlier talk with Bean, Chaplin had suspected stubbornness was one of Bean's strongest traits. And he had suspected equally that forgiveness was one of the weaker ones. Everything depended upon whether or not Bean had a sense of humor. But first he had better hope that Bean would even talk to him.

He rode alone toward the fort refusing Parmer's offer of an escort. He held his hand upraised as he rode, and he kept yelling, "Ellis. Ellis Bean. It's Chaplin. I want to talk to you." He wasn't sure his voice carried, but his attitude could be recognized.

A rifle bullet geysered dirt a half-dozen yards in front of his horse, and the rolling report of the shot drifted to him. He flinched but kept his horse moving forward.

"Bean, I want to talk to you." That effort tore the lining of his lungs.

The next shot was much closer, slamming into

the ground almost between the horse's forelegs. It reared, and the unexpectedness of it almost unseated him.

He forced the animal back to the ground. "Bean," he roared.

A volley of shots answered him, and they weren't warning shots. One plucked at his coat sleeve, and another whispered its nasty, little message into his ear. He whirled his horse and fled.

Parmer was grinning when Chaplin reached him. "Unfriendly cuss, isn't he?"

Chaplin looked back at the fort. Those shots had been his answer as to how Bean felt about the whole episode.

"He will be," he said grimly.

Bean stomped about the room raving with every step. "Who the goddamned hell do they think they are?" he yelled. "Firing on me and chasing me all the way home?"

Harter grunted something and reached for the bottle. The lowered level showed how drunk he was.

"By God, I couldn't believe my eyes when they came charging and shooting," Bean raged. "Dust all over the horizon. They must have thrown a couple of hundred men at me. So they don't even want to talk to me. I can kick some spokes out of their wheels." He turned a glowering regard on

Harter and snatched the remaining whisky out of his reach. He was tired of the man. Maybe kicking his ass out of here might vent some of his temper.

He stared at his guest. Harter looked like a gentleman, a dissolute one to be sure but still a gentleman. He might have his uses. He might be exactly the one to keep Ellis Bean informed about what was happening in Nacogdoches.

He said, "Harter, when you sober up I want you to ride into Nacogdoches. You sell yourself to Edwards. Tell him you hate the Mexicans. And you keep me informed about every move he makes."

Harter stared at him with bleary eyes, and Bean sighed in exasperation. He'd have to wait until Harter was sober, then repeat everything.

His pacing about the room became slower as calmness returned to him. He'd show that madman in Nacogdoches a few things. Edwards thought he was pretty secure because he had talked to Hunter. Hunter didn't have nearly the Indian support he thought he had, and what he held could be weakened. Bean cackled in obscene mirth. Bowles was the one to work on. Reports said that Bowles was sulking because he hadn't been invited to the Nacogdoches conference. Fields and Hunter had made a big mistake there.

He stopped his pacing, and his head cocked to one side. He was a tough, little man with a burning anger. Nobody humiliated Ellis Bean.

"I'd better send some gifts and whisky to Bowles," he said aloud. He could make as many promises as Edwards could. He could promise Bowles all the land he wanted. Bowles would leap at the chance to become the top chief of them all.

CHAPTER NINETEEN

A month can make a tremendous difference in a man's life, Chaplin thought moodily—or in a town's. Thirty days ago Nacogdoches was a bustling, growing town with a right to its forward look of optimism. New arrivals had filled its streets, and business was booming. Today the trend of traffic had reversed itself, and some of the stores were closed and boarded up. Very few married men remained for their family's safety was the primary thing. The town wasn't deserted. Groups of armed men lounged on the streets, and a casual glance would see only men lazying in the weak warmth of the December sun. But a closer inspection would see the alertness in their eyes, and the nervous manner with which they greeted each new and unexpected sound.

Traffic was still in the streets, but it wasn't the traffic of commerce. This was the traffic of war with scouts galloping out on missions and other scouts racing in with new reports.

Thirty days ago the major irritations to Nacogdoches were administrative. Today the irritations had a physical aspect, a menacing, physical one. The air was filled with conflicting rumors. Some said the Mexican army hadn't marched yet, that it would never march. Others said it was already at San Felipe de Austin and swelled to awesome numbers by Austin's and De Witt's settlers. A man couldn't depend upon the veracity of any single report. All he could do was make a choice and hope it was the lesser of the evils.

It was six days until Christmas, and Chaplin thought nostalgically of the Christmases in Louisiana. Great trees reaching to the ceiling would be in the parlors, and the shine in children's eyes would equal the shine of the ornaments and candles. He would be shopping now for something for Talitha, but he would have well-filled stores from which to select a suitable gift. Here a man was pressed to find anything but the ordinary needs of life. He had been fortunate to find the hand-carved ivory comb and the black lace mantilla for her. He hoped she would be pleased. He had fretted over the wrapping, and coarse, brown paper was the best he could do. The gifts would be better unwrapped. He would simply have to hand them to her and say, "Merry Christmas, Talitha." She had asked him a dozen times what he wanted, and each time he had been tempted to say, "Bullets." He believed a man wouldn't be able to get enough of them.

It was going to be a bleak Christmas for Haden

Edwards too. He hadn't heard from Natchitoches, and Hunter hadn't returned as he had promised. The thirty days Hunter had spoken of were almost gone. Each day Haden saw more men slipping away. Parmer and Ben had estimated two hundred of the farmers would join up. The farmers weren't joining, and even some of the Regulators were abandoning Parmer's command. Chaplin thought Parmer would be hard-pressed to raise two hundred men in all. No wonder Haden was like a bear with a sore head. The pressure was bowling him physically and spiritually, and he couldn't talk in a calm voice.

He hadn't been at all impressed with Chaplin's report of the chase of Ellis Bean. "Haven't I got enough to worry about?" he had shouted. "I don't give a damn what Bean feels or thinks."

Chaplin had wanted to say, you might give a damn one of these days. Bean had impressed him as a resourceful, cunning man—and a proud one. That pride might demand compensation.

Only Ben and Parmer were cheerful. They were in their element and were as happy as children with new toys. They chattered over each new report and spent hours moving armies about on paper. Chaplin wondered if the ghosts of great generals watched in openmouthed admiration. Parmer and Ben never lost a paper battle.

He walked into the office, and he hadn't seen Haden look this jubilant in days.

Haden waved a letter at him and shouted, "I just heard from Roberts. He's having great success in raising volunteers. He says they'll be ready to move shortly." He banged his fist on the desk. "We're going to win this thing, Chichester."

Chaplin's face brightened. Maybe the tide that seemed to be running against them for so long was turning. He said, "Now if Hunter comes in with a favorable answer—"

"He will," Haden said brusquely. His tone said he wouldn't allow it to happen any other way.

Hunter came into town the following day and brought a dozen chiefs with him. He wasn't smiling, but he was closer to it than Chaplin had ever seen him.

Hunter shook hands all around the office and said to Chaplin, "Bowles didn't come. When my Indian nation is formed, and his people find out how he led them they'll desert him."

He saw the question in Chaplin's eyes and snapped, "I can raise five hundred braves without him. They'll be here anytime they're needed."

Chaplin sighed in relief. He had been afraid Bowles' defection would lessen the number Hunter could supply. Add the Natchitoches volunteers to the Fredonian force plus the Indians, and they had a formidable force. For the first time in many a day he felt an overwhelming burst of optimism. Now he could join with Haden and say with conviction, we're going to win this thing.

"It's time to draw up our declaration of war and send a copy of it to Saucedo," Ben said.

Parmer agreed with enthusiasm, and Hunter nodded and said, "The sooner the better."

Chaplin leaned against the wall and listened to them wrangle over the wording. He wondered why official documents had to be so pompous and high-sounding? If you thought a man a bastard wasn't it more honest to say so rather than refer to illegitimacy or lack of the sanctity of the church? But makers of official documents were never happy unless they could use jargon that the ordinary man would have trouble in understanding.

He was weary of listening by the time the first paragraph was finished. Ben read it to the assemblage in sonorous tones. Ben Edwards was proud of this declaration, for most of it came out of his head.

He cleared his throat and began:

"Whereas the government of the Mexican United States have by repeated insults, treachery and oppression reduced white and red emigrants from the United States of North America now living in the Province of Texas within the territory of the said government, into which they have been deluded by promises solemnly made and most basely broken, to the dreadful alternative of either submitting their free born necks to the yoke of an imbecile, faithless and despotic government, miscalled a Republic, or of taking up arms in defense of their inalienable rights and asserting their Independence. They, viz; the White emigrants now assembled in the town of Nacogdoches, around the Independent Standard on one part, and the Red emigrants who have espoused the same Holy Cause, on the other, in order to prosecute more speedily and effectually a War of Independence, they have mutually undertaken, to a successful issue, and to bind themselves by the ligaments of reciprocal interest and obligations have resolved to form a Treaty of Union, League and Confederation."

He stopped and looked about the room.

Chaplin thought dourly, does he expect us to break into applause?

Hunter said with quick suspicion, "It says nothing of the guarantee of land to the Indians."

Ben gave him a reproving look. "I'm getting to that." He shoved the paper and pencil to Haden. "Write what I say." His eyes were fixed on the ceiling, but Chaplin suspected no mere boards would stop Ben Edwards' vision from going far beyond them. He knew a quick, stabbing curiosity. What did Ben Edwards see himself as—king, emperor, or merely president of this new republic?

Ben said, "One: The contracting parties bind themselves in a solemn Union, League and Confederation, in Peace and War, to establish and defend their mutual independence of the Mexican United States."

He stopped for a breath. "Two:—"

This could go on until Ben Edwards ran out of words, and Chaplin knew how long that would take. "Oh, my God," he exclaimed and pushed off the wall.

Haden gave him a pained look, and amusement glittered in Hunter's smoldering eyes. Parmer grinned, and Ben said coldly, "These things have to be done officially."

They didn't have to be done with him here. Chaplin wondered what the Indians thought of the white man's treaties. He imagined Ben would have been shocked by the thoughts behind those stolid faces.

He said, "If anybody wants me I'll be in the tavern." As he stepped through the door he heard Ben say, "Haden, he needs controlling. He gets more difficult every day."

Chaplin grinned sourly. He would bet that every man in the room with the exception of Ben would join him if they had the chance.

He walked in and ordered whisky. The humorous side of it struck him, and he grinned.

He wished he could see Saucedo's face when he got a copy of that document.

A man sidled up to him and said, "Pardon me."

Chaplin cut his eyes at him. He had never seen him before. He was dressed like a gentleman, but his clothes were in sad repair and in lack of cleaning. He had a thin, indefinite face and vague eyes. Chaplin noticed the trembling in the man's hands. He would say the man was used to whisky and that he was in need of a drink.

"You're pardoned," he said dryly.

"I'm Joseph Harter." He thrust out a limp hand. "Once a doctor."

Chaplin wondered why Harter put it in the past tense. A doctor's knowledge wasn't something that could be easily misplaced.

"Chichester Chaplin," he said and took the hand. "Why aren't you a doctor now?"

Harter held up his hands, and the shaking was apparent. "Would you believe that these hands were once as steady as a rock? They did that to me."

Chaplin asked, "Will you join me?" and nodded at the whisky bottle.

Harter accepted eagerly. He put down two shots before Chaplin could blink. This was a hard-drinking man.

"Who's they?"

"The Mexicans." Harter's eyes blazed. "They put me in prison for no reason. Oh the torture—"

He winced and reached for the bottle. He drank and breathed out gustily. Chaplin leaned back to escape the fan of the whisky-laden breath. "But I escaped. How I ever made it through their cursed country—" Harter stopped and shook his head.

"You're safe enough now."

"I won't feel so until I reach the States. But first I'd like to talk to Haden Edwards."

"Why?" Some instinct in Chaplin quivered and breathed life. This man was a stranger, an unlikely candidate to be seeking land, and yet the first one he asked for was Haden Edwards.

Harter smiled faintly. "Because I have information about the Mexicans that could be useful to him. I'd do anything to get revenge for their persecution."

The instinct was stronger. According to Harter's story he had struggled to get out of Mexico. And yet he seemed to know a great deal about local politics. Would he have learned about them on the way here? It was an interesting question, and Chaplin considered it. Could the man mean Edwards physical harm? Chaplin dwelt on that, then rejected it. He thought Harter was an unlikely type to send as an assassin. He could refuse to take the man to Edwards, and somebody else would. No he'd better do it and keep an eye on him.

He said, "Haden's tied up now." He thought of Ben's long-windedness. "It'll be at least an hour before he's free. I'm Haden's son-in-law."

Harter wrung his hand again, this time eagerly. Chaplin sighed. Maybe events were making him too suspicious for his own good.

They passed the hour talking and drinking. Chaplin's earlier suspicions kept fading. Harter was an educated man with an engaging manner. He knew the big cities of the south well, and he told amusing stories about them.

"Let's go see if he's free," Chaplin said. Perhaps the whisky had warmed him, but he felt friendly toward Harter. Any man who could drink and talk as well as Harter did had to be on the right side.

Haden and Ben were in the office when they entered. Ben looked at Chaplin, and his face was stiff. Ben was an unforgiving man, and Chaplin didn't give a damn.

"It's done," Haden said. "Copies are on their way to Saucedo and Austin. Hunter's returned to the villages to bring back—" He frowned as Chaplin made a gesture cutting him short.

Maybe the gesture was foolish. Half of Texas already knew Haden's plans, but still it seemed unwise for Haden to talk so freely before a complete stranger.

Chaplin ignored Haden's frown as he introduced Joseph Harter. "He wants to talk to you."

He listened again to Harter's story, listened with a critical ear. The only jarring note he could detect was that it sounded almost exactly the same as Harter had told it to him. Perhaps he was being too

212

picky, but would a man tell a story twice in the same sequences and using almost the exact wording unless it was memorized?

Haden didn't pick up any jarring note. He was fascinated after a few sentences. When Harter spoke of streets and landmarks in Mexico City Haden nodded. He knew those places well.

Harter said, "The Mexicans in San Antonio are panic-stricken at the fear you will revolt. The Mexican army wants no part of facing American rifles. I think they will turn and run at the first shot. The government in Mexico City is fighting for its life. It is in no shape to come to Saucedo's aid."

Ben said exultantly, "I knew it," and Haden's eyes gleamed with pleasure.

Chaplin wondered how Harter knew so damned much about the Mexicans in San Antonio. He had been trying to escape the country. Wouldn't he have given the populated centers a wide berth? Still fear in high places had a way of radiating down to the most obscure corners. Any peon could have given Harter this information.

I'm too critical, Chaplin thought. Ben and Haden accepted the man at face value. Suppose Harter's story was a complete lie. What real harm could it do? It wouldn't change the course of the war, it wouldn't stop or postpone the preparations. If anything, it would increase the intensity of them for the enemy was weaker than Haden and Ben supposed.

Harter stood and said, "If I could get a meal and a night's rest I'll be on my way to Natchitoches."

"You're in no shape to be traveling," Haden protested. "You'll rest more than a night."

An idea had been forming in Ben's head, and it glistened in his eyes. "You say you're a doctor?"

Harter held out his right hand. He clasped his wrist with his left hand to control its shaking. "I was."

"You are," Ben corrected. "I need a surgeon for my army." He hammered at Harter's protests and beat them down. "If you can't do it you can tell somebody else how to. You've got the knowledge."

Very few people stood before Ben's obstinacy, and Harter sighed. "I can try."

"Sit down," Ben ordered. "Here's what we plan to do. If we march on San Antonio and catch Saucedo's army outside of it, what will happen?"

Harter considered it a moment, then said slowly, "You'll cut them to pieces."

Chaplin moved to the door. He looked back, and the three had their heads together. Ben was laying out his campaign plans, and Harter agreed with every point.

They had accepted Harter on his words, and Chaplin had always believed a man's words were poor credentials. None of them noticed him glowering at them. Was he turning into a professional worrier?

CHAPTER TWENTY

Ellis Bean's eyes glistened as he finished reading Harter's report. He knew everything the Edwards brothers intended to do, and he picked at the hidden weaknesses in their plans. At the moment they were very weak. Hunter hadn't brought his Indians into Nacogdoches, and none of the volunteers from Natchitoches had arrived. The trick was to keep all the forces Haden Edwards depended upon from joining. Right now there were less than fifty Regulators in Nacogdoches. The Carancahuas Indian uprising in the Aes Bayou district couldn't have come at a more fortunate time. Ben had taken a hundred men with him to put it down.

Bean thought savagely, I could take Nacogdoches with fifty good men. He wished he had them.

Sergeant Mendoza came into the room and said with visible alarm, "Señor, a great body of men approaches."

"How many?"

Mendoza's eyes rolled. "A thousand."

Bean swore at him for the exaggeration. Nobody in Texas had gathered that many men.

He walked outside and looked over the wall. The sun was riding low on the western horizon, and for a moment he didn't spot the dust. He watched it with narrowed eyes. It took a lot of men to raise that much dust, but Mendoza's figure was ridiculous.

The dust cloud moved much nearer. Its makers were riding leisurely, and the first thought that flashed into Bean's mind was that Haden Edwards was moving up in force to attack Fort Teran. He discounted that immediately. This force wasn't coming from the direction of Nacogdoches. Fort Teran sat out in the open, and there was no advantage of swinging around to hit it from any particular direction. No, he decided. Those weren't Edwards' men.

"Get your men ready, Sixto," he said.

"Señor," Mendoza wailed. "Against so many? We would not have the chance."

"What do you want to do?" Bean snarled. "Run before you even know who they are?"

Regardless of who those men were he intended defending his place. He could muster thirty men, and the walls would give them a tremendous advantage. He could hold off three times as many as the approaching riders—if he had stouthearted men.

He listened to Mendoza giving weak-kneed orders. He didn't have those kind of men.

He kept his eyes riveted on the oncoming riders. A thousand men, he thought and snorted. He'd say they were less than a hundred. But the tenseness wasn't going to leave him until he knew who they were.

He yelled for his spyglass and focused it on the distant men. He swept it along the line of them studying each face for an instant. His sigh had relief in it.

"You can relax, Sixto," he yelled and gave Mendoza a bleak grin. "That's Norris and Sepulveda out there." He had no fear of them. He'd never had any quarrel with any of the outlaws. He wondered idly where Gaines was. Perhaps he had missed him in the pack.

Norris tied a white handkerchief on a stick and waved it as he rode. Bean watched him with a frosty grin. Norris was taking no chances of the fort being on the edgy side.

Bean was standing outside the wide, double doors when Norris rode up. Norris looked tired, and his mouth drooped sullenly.

"Light," Bean said. "What's the army for?" His eyes had grabbed a quick count. Eighty men, if he hadn't missed a few. Probably all the outlaws left around here. Wouldn't Haden Edwards be jubilant if he had a chance to smash them with a single blow.

"We need water and food," Norris said. "Can you supply us, Ellis?"

"If you pay for it," Bean said calmly. "I've got some grain and dried meat. I'll let you kill a beef."

"Set a price," Norris said angrily.

Bean set the price he wanted, and Norris

seemed too dispirited to haggle. He turned his head and yelled, "Get down. And I want guards out."

"What's the matter, Sam?" Bean jeered. "You seem a mite nervous."

"Don't prod me," Norris warned and strode by him into the fort. He said over his shoulder, "Do I have to pay for a drink too?"

"I always got a drink for my friends. You know that."

Bean poured the drink and watched Norris gulp it down. A man always drank this way when he had trouble riding heavily on his shoulders.

"What's the army for, Sam?" he asked casually.

"José and I raised them," Norris said. The sullenness had returned to his face. "We promised them loot, and I can't find any. There's no more traveling because of the war scare. All we're finding is a few deserted cabins. Not worth the trouble of entering."

Bean grinned. Sam Norris had never been too sharp-witted a man. With his sources of revenue cut off he had gone back to the old ways. And the old ways were gone.

"Jim pulled out?" Bean said.

Norris cursed Jim Gaines until he ran out of breath. "How'd you know that?" he demanded.

"Because he isn't with you." Jim Gaines was too smart to ride a losing cause. He'd sit out this war, then move in and pick up the spoils after it was over. Maybe he had advised Norris to do the same thing. If he had Norris hadn't taken it.

Norris held out his glass, and Bean refilled it. "You're having trouble holding them," Bean said.

Norris stared at him. Bean always had an uncanny knowledge.

"You've got to find something profitable and quick, or they'll be drifting away on you. I know just the job."

Norris leaned forward, the eagerness starting in his eyes. "What?"

"Nacogdoches."

Norris forgot his respect for Bean and swore at him. He'd been in Nacogdoches one time too many as it was.

Bean's face remained calm. "If you'll shut up and listen I'll tell you something. Ben Edwards' got a big bunch of Regulators out in the field. There's only about fifty men in Nacogdoches right now. The rest are on their farms, and it'll take time to collect them. You got enough men to carry the town. That'd give you enough loot to hold them."

Norris breathed hard and discovered his hand was trembling. God, he'd like to smash that town; he'd like to wipe it off the map.

"You telling me straight?" he demanded.

"Straight," Bean said solemnly. "I know every time Haden Edwards blows his nose."

Norris didn't question the reliability of the

information; he just questioned Bean's intentions. "What's in it for you?" he asked suspiciously.

"Not a damn thing. I'm just sick of seeing Haden Edwards mismanage things. And I don't want the Mexican army tramping all over Texas." His voice took on a sly note. "You'd stand pretty high with Saucedo if you ran Edwards out. You might even wind up with his grant."

Norris' eyes glistened. By God, Bean was right. Saucedo would be indebted to him if he wiped out that mess at Nacogdoches. It could make Sam Norris a big man, a much bigger man than Jim Gaines had ever hoped to be. He remembered the thousand and one little abuses Gaines had heaped upon him. He might let Gaines keep his land. He'd have to consider that for a long time.

"Get out that dried meat," he said. "We're riding tonight."

Bean frowned. "You'd be better off waiting until morning." A daylight attack was never smart. And tonight's ride would put Norris against Nacogdoches sometime in the morning.

Norris said impatiently, "We'll grab a couple of hours sleep on the road."

Bean looked at the glitter in the man's eyes. He had sold him too well. Norris couldn't wait to get started. That part was all right if Norris had enough sense to hole up outside Nacogdoches until dark. Bean decided Norris wouldn't be able to stand the long hours of waiting.

He tried to argue with the man about his timing, but it was useless. He finally stopped and ordered dried meat distributed among Norris' men.

He watched their animated faces as they discussed the coming attack. Every one of them felt as though Nacogdoches belonged to him, that he had been driven out. And every one knew how well-stocked the stores had been in the past few weeks. All those supplies were still in the stores. It made a man drool just to think about them.

They were a motley, savage-looking crew, and bloodshed meant nothing to them. How hard would they fight if the odds got tough? And could they carry the town against the defense of lesser numbers? Both of those were very interesting questions. Bean sighed. He would have to wait until at least tomorrow night for the answers. Because sometime tomorrow as sure as hell Norris was riding into Nacogdoches.

The early January sun was weak, giving more the illusion of warmth than the actuality. Chaplin lounged with Parmer in the square, taking full advantage of the sun. Haden was off with Ben in Aes Bayou. Chaplin thought resentfully, Haden had too much sublime confidence. He had stripped Nacogdoches of its defenses, saying that it was too early for anything to possibly happen. Parmer would be hard-pressed to raise twenty fighting men. The rest of his Regulators were still

221

scattered on their farms, and Chaplin believed it was past time to collect and have them ready. Haden was too practical. If he assembled his army the problem of feeding it was his. And until he called them that problem was the individual's.

Parmer looked at a scratch on his hand and said, "I don't believe that Harter knows a damned thing. I think this thing is infected."

Chaplin asked in a disinterested voice, "What did he do for it?"

"He smeared some kind of ointment on it," Parmer grumbled.

At the far side of the square Hunter was assembling the dozen Indians he had brought with him for the trip home. Chaplin thought Hunter would never leave Nacogdoches. The town had fascinated the Indians, and each day they had found some new item to delight them. They were going back loaded with gifts. That had cost Haden a pretty penny.

"The Yokum brothers going back with them?" Chaplin asked.

Parmer nodded. "Maybe they can hurry them along a little." He grinned and added, "If an Indian can be hurried."

A sense of urgency had been building in Chaplin for days. But apparently no one else felt it. He wanted Parmer's Regulators assembled and here, he wanted to see Hunter's five hundred braves, he wanted to count the volunteers from

Natchitoches. Everything was static now, and he craved action. He had no doubt that Saucedo was somewhere on the road by now. The smart thing would be to have Saucedo under observation, to have time to pick the spot of battle. They didn't have an inexhaustible amount of time though everybody acted like it.

Parmer tensed and straightened as he saw a rider coming toward town. "Something's happened to make him come that hard," he said.

They were waiting for the man when he arrived in the square. "Norris," the man panted. "And a hundred of the outlaws. I saw them coming and got out of my place in time. They threw a million bullets at me."

"You're not dreaming, Moseby?" Chaplin asked.

Moseby's face was indignant He had barely escaped with his life, and Chaplin asked him if he was imagining things.

"You wait," he threatened. "You'll see."

Parmer had hold of the bridle. "You want to help defend the town?"

Moseby looked about the square. "With what you've got here? You haven't got a chance. I'm getting out. I've stayed too long as it is." He pulled on the reins, jerking the bridle from Parmer's hand. He set spurs to the tired animal, and it lunged forward.

Parmer watched him until he was out of sight. "We got a lot of those kind."

Chaplin shook his head. "Too many."

It didn't take long for confirmation of Moseby's words to reach them. At first there was only a trickle of settlers fleeing before Norris' advance, then they came in a steady stream. Parmer asked each man if he wanted to stay, and the negative answers were overwhelming.

Parmer's voice grew more grim with each refusal. "Then just keep right on going," he growled to the last one. "I don't want you in the way."

"How many did we pick up?" Parmer asked.

"Six." Chaplin's eyes were on the horizon. That dust cloud out there wasn't imagination.

A familiar flame danced in Parmer's eyes. "Can we make it do?"

Chaplin gave him a tight grin. "Looks like we'll have to." It would have to be a clever and successful ambush to have any chance of success. If Hunter threw his handful of Indians into the battle at the right moment it could have a devastating effect.

"Let me talk to Hunter," he said. "Maybe those Indians would like to prove they're ready to fight."

"Talk good. We sure as hell need them."

Hunter listened woodenly as Chaplin talked. Chaplin said, "Hit them after we stop them. You can have everything they've got. Horses, rifles, clothes."

Hunter turned and said something in native tongue to the Indians. It took only a brief moment, but Chaplin thought it lasted an eternity.

"You stop them," Hunter said abruptly. "We'll join in."

"Good," Chaplin answered. He hoped his face didn't show the limp relief he felt.

He moved back to Parmer. "They'll join us."

Parmer nodded. "We'll defend from Stone House. That'll give us full coverage of the street and square."

That was the place Chaplin would have picked. Norris would enter by the main street for it was the only one that didn't dead-end against a stone wall or pasture fence. The street narrowed as it reached the center of town. Just before it reached the square ten horsemen couldn't ride abreast in it. A brutally, unexpected volley would pile up horses and men there. And panic would start at that spot.

"I've got men out collecting all the guns they can find," Parmer said. "I'd like to have three or four rifles to a man."

Chaplin gave him credit for being a good tactician. That first volley would be continuous and murderous. Not very many men would ride on in the face of it.

Twenty-two men gathered in Stone House. Each man cradled a rifle. Two more leaned against the wall beside them.

Parmer turned to Bill English and said, "Bill, go

to the edge of town and keep an eye on them. Get back in here in time for us to be ready."

English nodded and slipped out the door.

The waiting was hard. Men talked in muted tones or not at all. Chaplin looked at the meager force. Haden Edwards' empire could stand or fall right here.

English came back into Stone House, and he was grinning. "They're in town by now. Hell, they act like they're on a picnic. They're not expecting anything at all."

"Good," Parmer said with grim satisfaction. He snugged a rifle butt to his shoulder and peered out a crack between stones.

Chaplin's vision was limited. He could only see where the street entered the square. He heard the thud of hoofs, and it had a cautious sound.

Come on, he prayed. Come on.

The first file of riders came into view. The hesitant quality was still there, but the deserted square should reassure them. Riders pressed against those in the van, and Chaplin saw the impatience in them.

The leading riders were convinced they would find no opposition in this town. They spurred their horses and yelled, firing random shots into the air.

"Now," Parmer barked.

That first volley was a murderously wicked thing. And at the short range nobody could miss. Horses reared and plunged, and others went down as though their legs had been kicked from beneath them. Chaplin heard screaming horses and screaming men as he searched for either Norris or Sepulveda. He saw neither and picked a freebooter out of the saddle with his shot. One moment the man's face was there, distorted with its yelling, the next it was in the street, shock leaving it blank and unknowing.

He grabbed up the second rifle and emptied another saddle. That was madness out there in the square. He smelled the raw reek of blood and manure and knew that some horse had been gutshot. Riderless horses galloped wildly around the square and in their panic crashed into mounted horses, the impact sending both animals down in a threshing heap. Several animals dragged men by the boot caught in the stirrup. Some of the men flopped with a disjointed lifelessness, but a couple of them tried to grab at the earth and screamed hoarsely for help.

The riders in the leading file attempted to turn to escape the withering fire, and that added to the panic. They were packed together in that tight street, and men sobbed and cursed and beat at each other trying to gain enough free room to put their mounts into a run.

Chaplin fired his third rifle, and his eyes were bleak. This was sickening slaughter. Norris' force was already badly decimated and still more fire poured into them.

Hunter picked that moment to throw his Indians into the fray. Their war whoop was ear-shattering as they poured across the square. They fired one volley, then dived on the nearest outlaws with flashing tomahawks.

"Hold it, hold it," Chaplin yelled. He didn't want any of Hunter's men hit. The jam at the mouth of the square was showing signs of breaking up. Evidently, the outlaws at the rear of the mob had spun their horses and were fleeing. It gave room to the savagely pressed men in the van. Their only thought was of flight.

Horses ran up on the heels of those in front of them and stumbled and fell. The braves were among the fleeing men and dragged several out of their saddles before the horsemen could get enough space to kick their horses into a gallop. Those tomahawks rose and fell with deadly efficiency.

The dust slowly settled, and the street was strangely quiet after the insanity of the last few moments. A few men moaned but not for long for the Indians dispatched them with cold-blooded efficiency.

Chaplin leaned against a wall breathing heavily. Out in the street the Indians were putting the finishing touches to the wounded. Norris had live men and dead men. There would be no in-between.

"We crushed them," Parmer said exultantly. "How many do you think we got?"

"I'd say thirty," Chaplin said slowly. The rest of Norris' men were riding pell-mell across the prairie. He doubted they would stop until their animals collapsed.

"Did you see Norris or Sepulveda?"

Chaplin shook his head. And he had been looking for them. They might be among the dead out there, but he doubted it. Their luck couldn't run that good.

"I'm afraid they got away. They probably let the others push in to see what would happen."

"It doesn't matter," Parmer said impatiently. "We broke their back today."

Yes they had done that. Norris no longer would lead an organized force. Each man would be only concerned with his personal safety, and that safety demanded he get as far away as he could from Nacogdoches.

"Those Indians are damned good fighters," Parmer said admiringly.

A faint shudder ran through Chaplin. He was visualizing what five hundred enraged braves could do. He hoped Hunter and the chiefs had a little control over them.

"We won a big victory here," Parmer said gravely.

They had that. It was too bad Haden was embroiled with Saucedo. If he wasn't all his troubles would be over.

"I hope the Mexicans are as easy to handle," Chaplin said.

"They will be," Parmer said contemptuously. "I'm going now."

The Yokum brothers started to follow Parmer, and Chaplin called them back. "See if you can get Hunter started. We want those Indians in town."

They nodded solemnly and moved outdoors.

Chaplin stared after them. Why did he feel as though a cold wind blew on him? So far they had won every battle. But the big one, the really important one lay ahead.

CHAPTER TWENTY-ONE

No Indians. No volunteers. Those four words were driving Chaplin crazy. And the same words were putting concern on Haden and Ben's faces, though Ben still talked in his high-blown way. Parmer wasn't worried, but he had come here merely for the excitement. Whichever way this thing went he was bound to get what he wanted.

Word had reached them that Saucedo had marched from San Antonio with two hundred men. Chaplin groaned every time he thought of it. Two hundred men in the Mexican army. It wouldn't have taken much more than a fearful face to rout them.

He glowered at the new red and white flag flying on its mast. Ben had insisted that the republic of Fredonia had to have its flag. Ben had all the trappings for a republic—except an army to defend it.

Haden still maintained that Austin would join him—or at the very worst remain neutral. Chaplin had tried to convince him he was wrong. Saucedo's line of march proved it. Saucedo was headed for San Felipe de Austin. Austin joined him or fought him—and Chaplin was quite sure Austin wouldn't do the latter.

He walked into the office and Haden and Ben and Parmer were engrossed as usual in their paper war. After the slaughter of the outlaws a tighter security was kept on the town, and that was an improvement. But the waiting was palling on the man in the street too.

Parmer looked up and said, "Old Laughing Boy, himself."

Chaplin grinned sourly. He guessed he had been a burr under all their saddles. "Any word from Natchitoches?" he asked.

Haden shook his head. "But I sent Harter to stir them up. He'll lead them back." He caught the shock on Chaplin's face. "He's the man for it," he said testily. "He hates the Mexicans. And he talks well. When he gets through telling them what he's suffered the volunteers will be galloping all the way here."

Yes Harter hated the Mexicans. He talked constantly of it. Maybe that was the false note in him.

Chaplin said hotly, "You still don't know very much about him. Why didn't you send me?"

"I couldn't spare you," Edwards snapped.

The waiting was too important, Chaplin thought bleakly. Haden wanted him to be a part of it.

"When did he leave?"

"Last night." Haden turned his attention back to the map Ben was drawing.

Chaplin stared at the three bent heads before he turned and left the office. Harter had a tremendous start. He doubted he could ever overtake the man, but he might reach Natchitoches before any real harm was done. He couldn't explain even to himself why he was so insistent that harm would be done. But it was a conviction that drove him. Haden would rave when he learned that his son-in-law had made an unauthorized trip, but Chaplin had listened to him rave before.

He said his good-byes to Talitha, and she clung to him.

"Four days, Talitha," he said patiently. "I'll be back by then."

"But is it necessary?" she wailed.

"I think it is," he said soberly.

He picked his horse for endurance and speed. He hoped to make Natchitoches in less than two days, and it would be a severe test for man and rider.

Elisha Roberts' eyes glowed as he looked at the assembled throng. At least two hundred and fifty men were gathered before him. He had succeeded beyond his wildest hopes. These were tough, adventurous men, and the promise of free land had drawn them. Roberts smiled faintly as he thought of how Haden Edwards would bellow when he learned Roberts had wiped out the administrative costs. But it would be a small amount to lose to save an empire.

The flames from the torches were whipped into a dancing frenzy by the chill January wind. Every man had a handbill passed out by Roberts. He had stated honestly what they could expect to find in east Texas, and it hadn't deterred them.

He raised a hand for silence. "We march in the morning." He waited until the yelling wore itself out. "We'll be in Nacogdoches in two days."

"Hey, Elisha," a voice called. "Are you going to open your store there again?"

"I'm going to open it," Roberts answered steadily. "And it'll be permanent this time."

When the yelling died down again he heard the sound of hard-running hoofs. He saw the rider beyond the radiance of the torches, a dim, fast-moving blur. For a moment he thought the man was going to ride through the crowd, then he threw off at its edge.

"Let me through," the man shouted. "News from Nacogdoches."

Men parted to give him passage, and Roberts reached a hand down to help him up to the platform. The man looked hard-used. His news must be of compelling urgency for him to drive himself as savagely as he had.

He panted, catching his breath, and the crowd waited in tense anticipation. "The revolution is dead," the man announced flatly.

The roaring was loud and sustained in its protest. Roberts had to shout to make himself heard over it. "Who are you?" he demanded savagely.

The man didn't shrink from the anger that rose all around him. "Joseph Harter," he said. "I left Nacogdoches two days ago. Haden Edwards has been exposed as a despot trying to set up a kingdom to enslave his own colonists. He never meant what he said about freedom. He wanted to get you out there and work you for his own profit."

"That's a lie," Roberts shouted.

"Let him talk, Elisha," a burly man in the front ranks said. "Then we'll take him out and hang him."

Harter said doggedly, "It's true. The Mexican government found out about it and is moving to crush him. Austin has joined the Mexican army making a force of six hundred men. Sam Norris has three hundred more ready to move on Nacogdoches. Edwards has only a few men holed up with him in Stone House. Do you want to throw your lives away for nothing?"

Roberts' jaw slackened. The words had the ring of truth. This man knew Nacogdoches, and he knew the men involved.

The crowd caught Roberts' expression, and for the first time an uneasy murmur ran through it.

"The settlers are negotiating with Norris and Saucedo for their safety," Harter shouted. "The Fredonian rebellion is crushed. You'd be smart to forget the name of Haden Edwards."

"It's a lie," Roberts said, but the former conviction was missing. He saw a few handbills flutter to the ground, and the solid cohesiveness of the crowd was breaking up into little segments as men discussed this new turn among themselves.

The first, tiny drift toward the rear appeared, a crack in the solidarity of their ranks, and more handbills fluttered to the ground.

"Wait," Roberts cried. "Let me verify it. I'll send a man to Nacogdoches, and—"

Harter gave him a pitying smile "Your man may ride straight into Mexican hands."

The drift became a tide that couldn't be stopped. Roberts stood there helplessly. He could yell himself hoarse and not turn them.

He looked at Harter and said bitterly, "You did a thorough job."

Harter gave him a fleeting smile and stepped down from the platform.

Roberts watched him cross the grounds and move toward the nearest saloon.

The torches still danced in the wind, but the meeting ground was desolate and empty. Discarded handbills made the ground almost white. Haden Edwards' hopes were a tender, young bud covered and blasted by the snow of those handbills.

Roberts walked back to his store, and his steps were heavy. He sat down behind his counter, and his eyes were brooding. He could find no self-blame in this. He had done all he could. That Harter was a liar. Haden Edwards was no despot. His dream was to free men, not to enslave them.

He turned his head as he heard the door open. He stared a long moment and said unbelievingly, "Chichester."

"Elisha," Chaplin said and came into the store. He looked drawn and bone-weary, and he didn't have to speak of the long, wearing hours behind him. He had made excellent time, he had cut hours off Harter's lead, but the dullness in his eyes said he knew he hadn't cut off enough.

"Harter got here." He made it a flat statement instead of a question.

Roberts nodded.

"I thought so. A man told me I might find you at the meeting grounds, but it was empty." He had picked up one of the handbills and read its glowing promise by the light of a torch. The emptiness of the grounds made the handbill a mockery, and he had let the paper flutter to the ground.

"He got here," Roberts affirmed bitterly. "He sent them all back to their homes." Rapidly, he told of the message Harter had brought.

The dullness in Chaplin's eyes was replaced by fire. "The goddamned liar," he said gustily. "Nothing he said is true. We whipped Norris and scattered the outlaws. Saucedo is marching with just two hundred men. If I can take that many from here—"

"Oh, my God," Roberts wailed. "I had two hundred and fifty ready to ride."

"Get them back."

Roberts shook his head at the enormity of the demand. "They've scattered. It'd take days, maybe weeks to gather them all again." He thought of all the hours of riding and talking. He had gathered his volunteer force by convincing a man here, two or three there. He couldn't do it all over—even if they would believe him.

"I doubt they'd listen to me again," he said slowly. "Now they won't know what to believe."

Chaplin's shoulders drooped. "I guess that's it," he said in a dead voice. "If Hunter brings up his Indians maybe we can still pull it off."

"You're not going back?"

Chaplin gave him a surprised look. "Why yes. After I do a job. Did Harter leave town?"

"I doubt it. He was headed for a saloon the last I saw of him."

"Then he'll still be there." Chaplin whipped his

coattails back and tucked them behind the butt of his holstered gun.

"What are you going to do?"

Chaplin's burning glance said it was a foolish question. He turned and walked out of the store, and Roberts followed him. He never quite caught up with Chaplin's long strides all the way to the saloon.

Chaplin brushed open the doors and stopped just inside. A dozen men were in the room, and Harter was at the far end of the bar laughing and talking to three companions. Roberts sidled past Chaplin and stopped against a wall.

Men must have read menace in that silent, lonely figure just inside the door for the laughter stopped on uneasy notes, and the talk hushed.

"Harter," Chaplin said. It wasn't said loudly, but it had carrying power.

Harter turned his head, and his face went white. "Wait a minute." His hands rose in a pleading gesture.

"Why did you lie to them?"

"I had to." Harter was having trouble keeping his voice from breaking. "Bean made me."

Chaplin said patiently, "You mean he paid you. He paid you to keep him informed of everything we did, then sent you here."

He needed no more confirmation than the guilt written on Harter's face.

He just stood there staring steadily at Harter.

The man's nerve broke under those merciless eyes. He uttered a hoarse cry and fumbled at his vest pocket. When his hand rose the derringer was almost hidden in it.

Thirty feet was a long range for the weapon. Chaplin heard its spiteful report and the small *thwock* as the slug buried itself in the wall a foot from his head.

He drew and aimed with deliberation. Harter was frozen in horror, and his eyes were enormous in a death-pale face.

Chaplin aimed between those eyes, and he wasn't an eighth of an inch off target.

The bullet slammed Harter backward, and his knees broke. He flung out an arm and caught the top of the bar. He hung there a shuddering instant, then slowly slipped to the floor.

Chaplin still held the smoking gun. He looked about the room and asked softly, "Any questions?"

Men shook their heads, and one of them muttered, "He tried to kill you."

Chaplin nodded and stepped outside. Roberts joined him and asked, "Do you want me to go back with you?"

It was a brave offer from a storekeeper, and Chaplin's hand rested briefly on Roberts' shoulder.

"Elisha, one man more wouldn't be a drop in the bucket."

He turned and strode away, and Roberts watched until the darkness swallowed the lonely figure.

CHAPTER TWENTY-TWO

Haden paced the office, and his agitation made his face look more haggard. "My God," he said for the half-dozenth time. "Why don't we hear from somebody?"

"You shouldn't have let Chichester go," Ben said. "With every man so important—"

Haden whirled on him savagely. "Let him go?" he yelled. "I didn't have the slightest idea where he was until Talitha told me."

"That young man needs disciplining," Ben said sternly. "Just because he's your son-in-law he thinks he can—"

He closed his mouth abruptly at Haden's fierce glance. Haden's nerves must be stretched thin.

Parmer watched them covertly. He had expected an open break between them before now. Ben's old man's mouthings would put anybody on edge.

Haden turned to Parmer and asked, "Any word from the Regulators?"

Yes, the break must be very near, or Haden would have asked the question of Ben. For Ben had sent sixty Regulators to scout Saucedo and the Mexican army.

Parmer winced every time he thought about it. Nobody in their right mind would send that large a force on a scouting mission. That many men were awkward to move and too easily discovered.

A few men could have been much better hidden and have brought information just as well as the larger number. And it would have left a hell of a lot more men in town to defend it.

"Just that one report," Parmer said. "Saucedo and Austin have left San Felipe de Austin. Five hundred men. Saucedo's got Colonel Mateo Ahumado heading his army. I've heard of him. A good man."

He saw Haden's knuckles standing out in white relief. Not too long ago they had luxuriated in an abundance of time. Now the luxury was all gone. How long would it take Saucedo to reach here? Three or four days on a forced march? He guessed that would be about right. Haden Edwards was looking squarely up against a steep, blank wall. It was enough to frighten anybody.

Haden resumed his pacing. "My God," he said again. "If I could hear from Chichester."

"Do you want me?" a voice drawled from the doorway.

Every head whirled toward him. Chaplin stood there with a grim half-smile on his face. His clothing was travel-stained, and he looked gaunt and tired.

Ben shouted, "You had no right to go off without telling us. You had—"

Parmer saw the thinning in Chaplin's mouth. Ben was damned close to being flayed with hot words.

Haden said savagely, "Shut up."

Parmer hid his grin. It was probably a lot more gentle than Chaplin would have been.

Injury replaced the shock in Ben's face. Now he would sulk. That was fine. Chaplin could report without interruption.

"You missed some meals," Parmer said.

"They were sort of scanty," Chaplin admitted. "I think I need a drink most of all."

Questions burned Haden's tongue, but he held them as he moved to his desk. He pulled out a bottle and glass and poured a stiff drink.

Chaplin didn't take the glass from his lips until it was empty. A shudder ran through him, and he said, "Ah."

Haden couldn't hold his questions any longer. "You saw Roberts?"

"I saw him."

Chaplin was uncommunicative, and that wasn't good, Parmer thought. Haden had better prepare himself for some bad news.

"When is he sending the volunteers?" Haden shouted.

Chaplin looked at Haden, but he wasn't seeing him. He was looking at something back of him.

"He isn't," he said slowly. "You sent the wrong man."

Haden's face was bewildered. "But in his last letter he said he was—"

"He collected two hundred and fifty men. They

were ready to ride. I said you sent the wrong man."

Some savage emotion lashed behind Chaplin's eyes. The effort he made to control himself was visible. "Harter lied to them. He said your rebellion was dead. The volunteers had scattered by the time I got there."

Haden went ashen, and a shakiness appeared in his hands. "But why?" he whispered.

"Bean. The man who wasn't important. He planted Harter here, and you picked him to send to Natchitoches."

Haden did some soul searching, and the agony of it twisted his face. "The dirty little bastard." His voice was barely audible. "I wish I could see Harter again. I wish—"

"You don't have to worry about that."

"Did you kill him?"

Now that was the most damned-fool question Parmer had ever heard. Anybody could look at Chaplin's face and read the answer.

Haden said pleadingly, "Couldn't we raise them again? If you went back and—"

Chaplin said as gently as he could, "I tried that, Haden."

Parmer said brutally, "You haven't got that much time."

Haden cast him an agonized glance. "If Hunter brings in his Indians we can still do it."

Maybe, Chaplin admitted. But it would be

cutting it too thin. The superiority of numbers needed to make it an easy victory would be gone.

Jed Stevens came into the office and said, "The Yokum brothers are on the way in. They're riding like the devil is clawing at their tails."

Were they bringing good news or bad? The answer to that would have to wait until they arrived. Chaplin glanced at Haden. Even the small waiting that was necessary was carving him to pieces.

Four men were waiting anxiously in the street when the Yokums pulled up. They sat their horses looking soberly at the group.

Before they opened their mouths Chaplin knew that Haden could forget about Hunter and his Indians.

But Haden had to hear it, he had to have it put into words. "Where's Hunter? When is he bringing his Indians?"

"Hunter's dead," Quincy said with brutal directness. "And his Indians are never coming."

Haden aged ten years in that moment. He looked exactly what he was, a tired man with the years crushing his shoulders. Now there was no dream to buoy him. He stared straight into the ugly face of defeat, and his spirit died under the confrontation.

"What happened?" he whispered.

"Bowles had him murdered," Eric said. "After he had Richard Fields killed. I tell you I never drew a free breath all the time we were in that village. The squaws and kids are starving, and the braves kept getting drunker. They were getting whisky from somewhere."

Bean, Chaplin thought. Ellis Bean. The little, unimportant man. All he had done was plant himself across Haden Edwards' path and turn into a solid mountain that couldn't be scaled or bypassed.

"The tribes quarreled among themselves." Quincy picked up the story. "Hunter tried to unite them." He shook his head. "He really believed in his dream of land for his people. But they were too blind to see it. That last day we were there I thought we had our death warrant. Hunter was still trying to make them listen to him. One of the old chiefs said finally, 'All of you go back to your white brothers where you belong.' He picked out two braves to escort Hunter and us out of the village. We rode a couple of miles with those Indians' guns at our backs." He shivered at the memory.

His eyes were far away and unseeing, and Chaplin knew Quincy Yokum was reliving that day again.

"They turned us loose then," Eric said. "They took Hunter with them."

Haden grabbed at a feeble straw. "Then you're not sure Hunter's dead."

Eric nodded. "We're sure. We doubled back and

put a glass on them. Those two braves took Hunter to a river. They shot him. Both of them. We saw him sink in the river. Then we got the hell out of there."

Haden let out a sound that was close to a moan. "I guess that ends it." His voice was stricken.

"Not by a long shot," Ben boomed. "We've still got close to two hundred men. Haven't we, Martin?"

"If we get our scouting force back in one piece we might be able to raise that many," Parmer said. His eyes were bright and inquisitive. "You planning on whipping Saucedo and Austin with a couple of hundred men?"

"Austin won't fight," Ben said positively. "He marched with Saucedo to make a show. He won't fight when he goes up against Americans. No American would."

Chaplin wondered how far their forces could be whittled down before Ben admitted defeat. Austin would fight. There was no doubt about that.

"We'll separate Austin and Saucedo," Ben said briskly. "Then we've only got the Mexicans to whip."

Chaplin thought he saw Haden's face beginning to brighten, and he said violently, "Goddamn it." He glared back at the eyes staring at him. When would any of them face reality?

He searched for words, and before he found what he wanted to say, Parmer said, "Rider coming in." He shaded his eyes, squinting to the south.

"Who is it?" Ben asked.

Parmer shook his head. "Can't make him out yet."

"One of our scouts," Ben said. He rubbed his hands together in pleased anticipation. "With a report on Saucedo. I'll bet he reports that Austin and Saucedo have split."

You fool, Chaplin thought angrily. That chilly, little wind was wrapping about him again, and that was odd, for the red and white flag hung limply from its pole. He had the ominous portent of final disaster, and maybe it was best. Haden's dream had been supported by the flimsiest of threads, and each had broken at the slightest pressure. The final thread was the false hope Ben had raised by saying they could pit two hundred men against Saucedo and win. Haden had to take every bitter step. He had to see the actual snapping of that last thread before he believed it.

Break it, Chaplin thought savagely as he watched the horseman approach. Break it and get it over with.

"It's Halverson," Parmer said, and there was a tightness in his voice. "He was with the scouts. He's coming damned hard."

Chaplin understood the tightness. A man riding hard always meant an emergency.

Halverson came into town, and he was weaving

in the saddle from exhaustion and loss of blood. The left front of his shirt was caked with dried blood, and his face had a white, dazed look.

Chaplin sprang forward to help him down. "You need attention," he said.

Halverson shook his head. "The hole's plugged up. I'm all right."

"Your report, man," Ben said impatiently. "What's happened?"

Halverson stared at him before he answered. "We got captured. Every goddamned one of us. We rode right into a trap, and the first thing we knew we were surrounded. Saucedo had a million men thrown around us."

Ben's voice was incredulous. "Didn't you try to fight your way out?"

"A couple of us made the wrong move. I got a hit in the shoulder. Purcell's dead. I guess we didn't have much heart in it. Saucedo had Americans in his army."

It was the final, ironic blow. Haden's men wouldn't fight against Americans. Austin's men did.

"I got a letter from Colonel Ahumado," Halverson said. "I wanted to bring it. He's expecting an answer."

Haden's fingers trembled as he tore it open. His face crumbled as he read it. He stood there as though he was frozen, and Chaplin thought, he's had enough time to read it a dozen times.

"What's he say?" Ben asked impatiently.

"He's holding our men as hostages," Haden answered dully. "They'll be released without harm if we get out of the country. He promised that Nacogdoches will suffer no damage, and that all of the titles I've given will be honored. If I give up all claims no one will be punished for conspiracy."

Chaplin sighed. It was an open pardon for all of them, a chance to leave the country without bloodshed. Only a man's dream would be destroyed. He looked at Haden's ashen face. And his heart, he added.

Ben laughed. "He's a fool. We can cut our way through and rescue those men. Ahumado won't be expecting it."

Chaplin's face turned raw and violent. "You'd jeopardize those lives—"

"That's enough, Chichester," Haden said wearily. His smile was only a ghost. "Even I know when the odds are impossible."

Ben's eyes burned with accusation. "You're giving up?"

He read the answer in Haden's face and turned and stalked to the flagpole. He hauled down the flag and tucked it under his coat. He moved heavily, but his back was ramrod straight. Ben Edwards had a shattered dream too, but Chaplin watched him without pity.

"We're the leaders Ahumado's talking about," Haden said. "It's every man for himself now."

He looked at Halverson, and his face had a tired dignity. "Tell Colonel Ahumado we're accepting his terms."

He turned and walked toward the wagon camp.

Parmer shrugged and said, "Guess I'd better saddle up."

Chaplin watched him cross the square. There was no depression in Parmer's stride. He had found the excitement he had come here seeking.

Chaplin moved slowly through the town to the encampment. Like the town, the camp was only a ghost of its former self. He heard no laughter, no voices, and great gaps were now in the once solid ring of wagons. He suspected the few remaining wagons would be gone by night.

He walked toward his tent. He had never built Talitha a house here, and the regret died before it was fully born. A tent was an impermanent, impersonal thing. A house would have been so much harder to leave. Maybe he was lucky that the days had been too full for him to start building. He thought, How long have we been here? and ran back over the months. Actually, by calendar time it hadn't been long, but it seemed like he had been here forever. Maybe a few of his smaller roots had entered Texas soil.

Talitha saw him coming and ran out to meet him. Her face was filled with concern as she cried, "What happened? Father wouldn't talk to me."

"He's pretty low right now. We're going home, Talitha. We're leaving Texas."

She asked in wide-eyed wonder, "For good?"

He nodded solemnly.

"Home," she said and tears filled her eyes.

He took her in his arms and let her cry. She lifted her face, and he ran a finger down a tear-streaked cheek. "He's lost everything?" she whispered.

"Everything here. He's got everything he had in Louisiana." It wasn't quite true. Haden had lost a fortune here, but he had the land in Louisiana, and the land had made that fortune.

Her eyes filled with sorrow for her father and before it could spill over again he said, "I'll bring up the wagon. Start packing."

He would rush her in the packing. He would keep her so busy she would have no time to dwell on her father.

He hitched the team and tightened the harness. Haden passed him driving a team and wagon toward town. Chaplin knew where he was going. Haden was going after his personal, movable items in Administration House.

Chaplin was surprised to find himself humming a little tune as he worked. Why not, he thought after a moment's reflection. A man couldn't bury himself in the past. As long as the excitement of looking forward coursed through a man he would always be alive.

Haden and Ben Edwards crossed the Sabine River on the last day of January. Haden pulled up and waited for Chaplin and Talitha. His eyes were bitter as he looked back into Texas. Haden had left a lot of himself back there, Chaplin thought. The springs that rejuvenated a man were drying up in him. Ben looked old and shrunken, and he hadn't opened his mouth so far. Chaplin knew a faint pity for him. For a while Ben had found his fountain of youth back there, and for a short period the illusion of its life-giving powers had sustained him. But the illusion had gone like smoke before wind, and now he was only a tired old man.

He'll have his stories to tell, Chaplin thought, and the pity vanished. He can sit and rock and tell how he almost won all of Texas.

Haden said, "They're fools, Chichester. Austin, De Witt—all the rest." The dream flickered briefly in his eyes and was forever dead. "I could have opened up a great, new country." He was silent a moment struggling with something that was hard for him to say. "Chichester, where did I make my mistake?"

Not one mistake, Chaplin thought. Dozens. Haden had made the mistake of impatience, of bulling ahead on unknown ground. He had no sensitivity of other men's feelings, and he had injured Saucedo and Bean. He had no ability to shade colors—everything was either black or white, and he trusted or rejected a man on that basis. Those were all mistakes, but the biggest of all was bringing Ben Edwards to Texas and turning over everything to him.

Chaplin looked at the tired old man sitting beside Haden. Recriminations wouldn't change a day back there. He said gently, "I don't see how you could have done a thing differently, Haden."

Haden sighed and picked up the reins, and Chaplin's words eased some of the pain in his eyes.

"I could have won Texas for them," he said. "They'll have to do it someday. You remember this. One of these days Austin and De Witt and all the others will have to do what I tried to do for them. I predict that in ten years they'll be fighting for their lives back there."

He clucked to the team, and the wagon moved on.

Chaplin looked back for the last time. He thought Haden was right. Americans had tasted Texas, and the longer they stayed there the more their craving for it would grow. To stay there they would have to fight Mexico for their freedom and land, for their very lives. The abrasive grinding between two different races had already started, and it could only grow worse. The gap between cultures, laws, and thinking could never be fully bridged.

Talitha looked at his sober face and asked, "What are you thinking about?"

"What Haden said." Haden was right. He could have done it for Austin and the others at a fraction of the cost. Right now men called him a madman. A few years could reverse that judgment.

"But he's wrong about a war starting in ten years. It'll start before then. I wonder if Austin will remember this time and wish it was back."

She said with a woman's insight into the future, "If it happens you'll come back and help them." Or perhaps she just knew her man well.

He smiled as he snapped the reins on the team's rumps. "I wouldn't be surprised."

KTE

Center Point Large Print
600 Brooks Road / PO Box 1
Thorndike ME 04986-0001 USA

(207) 568-3717

US & Canada:
1 800 929-9108
www.centerpointlargeprint.com

Pennell @ my

RV 11.13

MG 12.13

BV 2.14

APK 10/16

KWF

JU

MDH 11/18

Good Read ✓